# Echoes of Treachery

## Veil of Shadows

### Book Eleven

## M. R. Pritchard

# ECHOES OF TREACHERY
## (VEIL OF SHADOWS 11)

**M. R. Pritchard**

**Meg has finally found love, family, and a life she never thought she deserved.** But just as she begins to embrace it, chaos looms on the horizon.

**The Safe Houses are burning, the horde of the dead swells, and the Veil between realms is thinning.** The Deacons, once protectors of order, are falling one by one. And the man who nearly killed her years ago—**the one who haunts her darkest nightmares—**may be returning to finish what he started.

Meg has spent her life deceiving Demons and Angels, outwitting even the most powerful beings in all the realms. But as her kingdom teeters on the edge of annihilation, her greatest weapon—her lies—might also become her greatest weakness.

With everything she loves on the line, **Meg must decide: will she face the truth or continue weaving the webs that could destroy her?**

Love, betrayal, and war collide in a battle for survival where secrets have the power to kill—and Meg may have to pay the ultimate price for hers.

# ONE



*MEG*

I'M SITTING on a soggy dock, feet dangling in cool, dark water, watching the loons floating in the morning mist. Nightingale runs toward me, sprinting on water, arms outstretched, terror etched on her face. The loons scramble away, their wings flapping against the water as they soar low. I want to yell at Nightingale for ruining my fucking peace. She promised to stop, but this must be something serious because she hasn't come to me in a dream like this in years.

"What is it?" I ask.

"Wake up, Meg." She's shaking my shoulders. "Get up! Get up now! Wake up! You must save your children!" she screams in my face.

My eyes flash open. I sit up in bed, smelling acrid creosote. It's familiar but too intense, too fresh. The window is open; no birds chirp, no owls hoot. There's fresh smoke drifting inside, the hammering of stone and metal, shouting echoes.

Skeele shifts, moving closer, smoothing his hand over my hip.

Someone howls like a creature of night out on a hunt. There are footsteps in the hallway.

"Wake up!" I yell to Skeele, launching myself out of bed.

He's on his feet, naked, ready to fight, a speck of dried blood on his lip. We wake to chaos. There's no slow morning stretches with our limbs rubbing together, no savoring the memories and ache of last night.

"Get dressed." I throw him a pair of pants and a shirt.

"The babies." His eyes are wide, terrified. "Get them." Skeele's shirt gets caught on his horns. He tugs hard, tearing it in a rush.

He calls them babies still but they are much older, too old to be called that. They're teenagers now, but he's never stopped. I guess compared to him, they will always be babies. Young, innocent, his–something he never thought he'd have. Skeele never thought he'd have a family. Neither did I. He was bred to serve the throne but took on so much more. I have always lived a life of chaos and destruction and never thought I deserved the love of a real family. Raised on the Earthen plane by a Demon who killed my mother, I knew nothing but feat and mistrust and hate. It took a long time to get to where I am now.

Dread spreads through my gut. Teari warned me of something terrible coming years ago. I threatened to kick her out of my realm because she didn't give me details. She just had a feeling, a premonition. She was right and now

I'm thankful she told us. Otherwise, I wouldn't have a bugout bag packed and ready, or a plan.

I grab clothes and throw them on. I get my bag, my blade, and other weapons.

"Here." Skeele tosses me the jar of Snowy Owl feathers from my bedside.

*Poof.* I leave the room.

"Children," I whisper, shaking them awake. "Wake up right now."

Remington launches up straight with a deep intake of breath. Rue wakes quieter. Green eyes flash open, her arms jerk to the sides, gripping the sheets. "Are we going to die?" she asks.

"Get moving." I throw her blankets back and don't answer her question. I can't answer because fear is more than a flood threatening to overtake my body. It's a tsunami, an earthquake, something thoroughly consuming that clogs my throat and traps my words. My children will not die. Not again. But I might.

This is not new. I have been attacked by evil before, but that was when my world was small. The stakes are higher than ever now. I couldn't protect the seed in my womb then, but now... now I could lose everything I didn't think I deserved. Fate has been cruel and unfair, but I don't have time to dwell on it.

Remington and Rue scramble out of bed, and when they smell the smoke that seeps under their door and hear the commotion echoing in the hall, they move quickly and meet me in their closet.

"Get clothes," I say. "Boots, knives, leather jackets, and pants."

They know what to do. Everything is within reach for a quick exit.

Clea arrives, wisps of white swirling into her ethereal form. "Let me say goodbye," Clea's voice breaks through before she's fully formed. "I must say goodbye to them."

My mother's lips are deep red, her transparent skin a ghastly white, but she doesn't scare them. This is all they know of their grandmother. She died the day I was born, so it is all I know of her as well.

"Hurry, Clea," I warn, collecting more clothing and tucking knives into Rue's pockets.

"Oh, children," her form turns solid, "be safe." She hugs them together, one on each arm, hugged so tight they might complain that they can't breathe, but instead they embrace her just as fiercely.

"What have you seen?" I ask Clea, tossing a pack to Remington. He straps it on and pulls the clips tight.

"Demons from the mountains. Lesser Demons from the south. Bugs and snakes and roaches coming in droves." Clea shivers with disgust. "The dark energy is strong, familiar."

"Did you see a face?" I ask, helping Rue tighten her pack so she can run if she needs to without it flopping around on her back.

"Not yet," Clea says. "I had to stop and say goodbye." She squeezes the children one last time. "I'll go back."

"Be careful," I warn.

"Hide them well," Clea says with a warm smile, patting each child on their cheek then pinching them. "I wish you could take my bones so I could go with you and have more time. Our women are cursed with losing children."

"They won't be lost," I say. "They'll be in hiding."

Clea nods and straightens her back. "Hurry." She turns toward the door. "Something is coming."

I nod. "Help the Hellions. Skeele is in charge while I'm gone."

For a split second, I wonder where my grandfather, Lucifer, put Clea's bones after I found them all those years ago. I make a mental note to add it to my to-do list then curse myself for not thinking of it sooner.

I take Rue's hand then Remington's. *Poof*–we're gone.

# Two

*BEFORE THE ATTACK ON THE CASTLE IN THE Burning Caves*

ALASTOR TREKKED from his hovel in the mountains to the Black River of Hell's Adirondacks. He had one goal: secure a Basilisk. He didn't have a castle to defend–yet– but he'd need the creature to get there. Lucifer had told him. Get the Basilisk, demolish the Deacons, feed the horde, storm the castle, kill everyone but Meg. Find his bones.

Alastor drove to Old Forge, taking Interstate-81 but avoiding all of Pennsylvania. He passed herds of the walking dead, a smirk crossing his face as he counted them and calculated how large his army would become. He didn't desire the throne, but the thrill of power was something Alastor couldn't ignore. He'd been thriving on it since growing the skin trades bigger than they'd been before Shay and that half-breed scum Jed had tried to take him down.

Yes, the intoxicating rush of power swelled within Alastor now; it swelled with need; more, more than ever before.

Alastor turned off the exit toward Interstate-481 north, then turned onto Interstate-90 east. He passed farmland and dense forests. He saw signs for the Safe House nearby. He made a mental note to have those taken down. Soon there would be no need for a Safe House or repenting because all souls would stay in Hell and *he* would dole them out to a realm or a Kingdom using his own deal with the Archangels.

Alastor merged onto 365 E and veered off onto Eastern Rock Road. The Jeep jostled across the busted parking lot, pavement cracked and sunken into the soft ground. He turned onto Moose River Road and drove past old houses and grocery stores. The Black River roared from nearby, the waters turbid and angry and the slick serpentine backs of the Basilisk blending in with the motion of the water.

They were spawning. Perfect.

Alastor parked his vehicle, tires snapping pine needles and releasing their scent. He got out and made his way to the edge of the riverbank. Standing on a giant rock, he planned the next move. There were plenty of ways to fish for a Basilisk. He needed the biggest one, though. Nothing small or weak. He needed a giant Basilisk that could consume an army.

Alastor jumped down to the lower rocks and made his way toward the shallow pool of baby Basilisk.

A giant head rose from the surface of the river, watching with a sinister gaze. Rows of sharp teeth flashed and a warning hiss echoed.

"Come on ya slimy bitch," Alastor said, pulling a knife from his belt.

He crouched, reaching into the pool of babies. The mother swam closer, teeth bared. Alastor reached into the water and grabbed a small one. An ear-piercing squeal signaled the mother. Alastor cut the baby in half and tossed the body back into the water, turning it a murky red. The mother moved closer, jaws gnashing, threatening. It didn't scare Alastor–he had a plan. Alastor jumped in the dark water and made quick work of slaughtering all the baby Basilisk. Within minutes, he was saturated in bloody river water. Alastor rubbed the pieces of Basilisk on his body, dipping his head and coating his hair and clothing in their blood. He bathed, rubbing their blood on his arms and neck.

The Mother Basilisk slithered closer, confused. Her children were dead, but Alastor smelled just like them. She glanced to the blood bath then the Demon. He smelled like them, like hers. He must be her child, the only one, the very last one. Being a creature of darkness, she would protect him until the very end.

Alastor tucked pieces of bleeding Basilisk into his pockets so the smell remained fresh. He emerged from the river, covered in blood and bits of flesh and bone. His clothing clung to his skin and bloody water dripped down his body in dark rivulets. He walked back to his Jeep, smiling as the Mother Basilisk followed him, a menacing shadow at his back.

# THREE

*Meg*

Peabody Library is dark. When we arrive, it sets off every ward in the building. After all these years Jed *would* ward his home against me. Typical Jed.

The horse shows up to investigate first. A shallow whinny greets us.

"Nero! Come clear this rune." I motion to the circle of salt and chalk that's trapping us.

Nero shakes his head in a firm response of "no."

The damn horse doesn't even trust me. Perfect. I can't blame Jed or Shay, I've gotten them in plenty of trouble over the years. They probably don't want any surprises.

"Go get Shay," I say. "And hurry."

Before the giant black stallion gets himself turned around, footsteps echo down the hall.

"Meg?" Shay's voice calls.

"Shhh," Jed shushes her.

"Come free us," I holler. "I don't have much time." I do my best to hide the panic in my voice. I have to get out of here, return to Hell and defend the castle.

"What shit-fuckery did you bring us this time?" Jed asks, rounding a bookshelf. He stops short when he sees the children behind me. His eyes go wide, knowing. "What's happening?" He moves closer but doesn't clear the rune.

"The castle in the burning caves is under attack." I shift on my feet, eager to get out of the circle in the middle of the room. I feel too exposed like this, trapped with my children. I want them hidden. I want them away from the door.

"You mean *your* throne is under attack?" Shay clarifies.

I nod.

Jed takes a few quick steps forward and scuffs his boot over the runes on the floor.

I take a deep breath and step away, dragging the children with me. I go to Shay. She helped me many years ago with a search and rescue. Then again, when the Deacons imprisoned me, she impersonated me to keep the throne of Hell safe.

"I need you to take them," I say, desperate.

"Are you sure about this, Meg?" Shay's voice breaks through my thoughts, concern clear in her eyes.

I nod, trying not to fall apart at the thought of handing my children over for someone else to ensure their safety. "I have to go back. The attack on the castle needs to be stopped, and I'm the only one who can do it."

"We'll take care of them," Jed says, stepping closer.

I swallow hard, fighting back the tears threatening to spill over. Turning, I face Rue and Remington, trying to ignore the ache in my heart. This might be the last time I see them. "Listen to Shay and Jed. They'll keep you both safe." I grip their hands and squeeze. "Promise me."

"I promise," they reply in tandem.

"A promise is a promise, remember?" I grip them in a tight hug.

"A promise is a promise," Remington repeats, the sound and tone of his voice too familiar to someone else's. Someone from my past. The one person who is probably on their way to kill me.

Rue's eyes well with tears as she clutches me with both arms. "Don't go," she pleads.

"I have to. I'll come back for you, I promise." I say, hoping it's not a lie.

Barely able to speak past the lump in my throat, I turn back to Shay and Jed. "Thank you," I muster.

With a last glance at my children, I turn and walk away, each step heavier than the last. The weight of my decision presses down like a boulder on my back. This is the right decision. It must be.

"Wait," I say. "One more thing." I drop my bag off my shoulder, unzip it, and pull out the jar of snowy owl feathers. "Put this somewhere safe. Please."

Shay reaches for the jar. It's small, not much more than a jelly jar; etched glass and a steel lid. These are the remains of my dead daughter, Elise. I swallow hard, tamping down emotion, afraid that this night might leave me with three jars of feathers and no children. I'm not sure I can go back to that person. Empty, filled with fear and hate. Three jars of feathers would most certainly release the monster inside me.

There. I have left everything that I care about in the

Peabody Library. Everything I never thought I'd have, I've left in the hands of others.

Jed and Shay are good. They will do what is right. They will protect my children. Jed has been on the run his entire life, he knows all the tricks. Shay was raised a prepper on a Montana ranch; she's the strongest woman I know–even stronger with the Demon poison that's embedded in the scar on her leg. Yes, mild relief flushes over me. This is the best place for them.

# FOUR

Shay took the jar of mottled white and brown feathers, blinked, and she was immediately transported back to a memory from a Crossroads Demon deal.

*The air crackled with an ominous energy as the figure approached the crossroads, their steps hesitant yet filled with a sense of desperate determination. They bore the weight of something heavy upon their shoulders, their gaze haunted by the specter of tragedy that loomed over their existence.*

*It was a Deacon.*

*Nero backed up.*

*Shay tensed.*

*Deacons were the gatekeepers of balance between the Seven Kingdoms of Heaven, the Earthen plane and Hell. Why did one summon Shay and Nero?*

*"What is it that you seek, Deacon?" Shay asked.*

*The Deacon hesitated, their gaze flickering with uncer-*

*tainty before they spoke, voice tinged with a mixture of power and desperation.*

*"No one can know that I'm here," the Deacon said.*

*Shay nodded. "Is that your deal?"*

*"No." the Deacon folded his hands. "This deal will be a great burden for both of us."*

*The Deacon kept looking over his shoulder and to the desert beyond. He'd drawn them to a crossroads in the middle of nowhere. They could see for miles even with only moonlight.*

*"There is a great darkness coming," the Deacon warned.*

*"That sounds like a warning, not a deal. Why did you call me here?" Shay didn't want to return to Alastor, but she didn't want her time wasted by this creature.*

*The Deacon paused and closed his eyes, finding calm and choosing his words carefully. "The deal is, you must take the children to safety and tell no one where they are. You must hide them until Clea's prophecy comes to fruition."*

*"What children?"*

*The Deacon held up a finger. "They are not born yet. When the time comes, you will know. You must agree to this now, before it's too late."*

*"What are you wishing to give me?" Shay asked, knowing that what the Crossroads Demon would take was not negotiable and typically unknown.*

*"I will give my life. Sooner rather than later."*

SHAY BLINKED AGAIN before glancing at Nero. His ear twitched with recognition. He remembered the deal.

"They'll be safe here. We won't let anything happen to them," Shay said.

Meg nodded, and Shay noticed the slight quiver in her bottom lip. Meg wouldn't fall apart though, never did. She always kept her feelings in check unless it was *anger*. That was a feeling she wasn't afraid to let out. She'd kept it tamped down since the children were born. Now love... That was a feeling Meg kept under wraps and Shay could understand why. Meg had let her love escape once; she'd loved the Raven King and he nearly killed her. He ruined her, wrecked her, let others clean up what was left of her broken heart and bleeding body. Meg was right to have trust issues. Last time she trusted someone heart and soul, she'd nearly died. Shay would never forget the moment Jed arrived, covered in blood, and panicking that they'd die in Hell along with Meg. When she had *poofed* back to Hell at Skeele's feet, the Hellions tried to save her and failed, so they dragged Jed into the mess. Jed did what he could, but he wasn't as strong a spell caster in those days. It was Teari's knowledge that brought her back to life. Since Meg would no longer get blood from Sparrow, her first in Command, Skeele, had to give her blood and it forced a bond that resulted in children.

Shay focused on the children standing behind Meg. They seemed despondent, didn't show a speck of fear. They'd never been to the Peabody Library, never been to the Earthen plane as far as Shay knew. Shay and Jed had known them their whole lives, spent time with them during the holidays and Sunday dinners that Meg held. Shay and Jed attended, both having no other family and feeling compelled since Meg bought the library and let them live there.

Shay reached out to Rue first and hugged her. She gripped Remington's shoulder and gave him a little shake as a greeting and a promise.

"We'll take good care of them, for as long as you need," Shay promised.

Rue didn't say a word, but Shay noticed the slight tremble of her bottom lip, exactly like her mother. She'd have to learn how to hide that better. The girl swiped at long dark hair that had fallen across her eyes.

Jed was there, taking Remington aside and whispering to him, no doubt warning him of the Earthen plane and what the boy could and could not do while he was here.

Shay shook Meg's shoulder, "If you've got to burn it all to the ground, then let it *burn*."

A chill passed through Meg as Shay's eyes flashed black. It was a side-effect of the Demon poison in Shay's leg. She was tethered to the Crossroads Demon Nero, her horse. As a result, Shay had the ability to transform into something wraithlike and make deals that transcended all the realms.

Shay tipped the jar to the side, watched the feathers drift, and realized that they looked very much like Meg's wings.

Meg nodded, tucking her wings tight against her back.

Shay hugged her, worried that Meg might fail. No. No. Shay wouldn't let that thought out into the wild. Never wanted it to become true. Meg was the strongest person Shay had ever met. Shay squeezed Meg tighter, easy not to pinch her wings.

"Burn it all, Meg," Shay whispered in her ear. "You are formidable."

Meg wiped her eyes; she wanted to tell the children goodbye again, but she'd been here too long. She needed to go back.

"One last thing," Meg said as she pulled a small piece of paper from her pocket and tucked it into Shay's hand. "No one knows about this place. Only myself and Skeele."

Meg raised a hand, gaze meeting her children's as she waved goodbye to them. Meg never prayed because she couldn't worship a God who'd allowed such violence and pain in her life. She couldn't see the worth in a being who allowed everything that had happened in her life. No, she'd never prayed but in that moment she did, and she prayed that it wouldn't be the last time she ever saw them.

*Poof* – Meg returned to Hell.

# FIVE



*BEFORE THE ATTACK ON THE CASTLE IN THE Burning Caves*

ALASTOR MOVED through the darkness of Hell with a singular purpose, his eyes burning with the intensity of his mission. The landscape of Hell, with its familiar chaos and torment, mirrored the turmoil within his mind as the voice of Lucifer drove him. Each step he took left scorched earth in his wake, a testament to the power that coursed through him. He distorted Meg's realm with each step.

The Safe Houses were his next target; sanctuaries for the lost souls to find their final resting place and the only place they'd find refuge from eternal torment. Within those walls balance was kept, and Alastor intended to snuff it out completely. No souls would leave Hell.

The Safe Houses began falling one by one.

Alastor began with the ones furthest away. Those that wouldn't be noticed until it was too late. It would upset the balance and sorting of souls, but the Seven Kingdoms of Heaven would blame Meg as they always did. She was an easy scapegoat and none would figure out the truth until it was too late.

Alastor found the eldest of the Deacons at the Safe House; he looked like no one and everyone, nondescript, neither short nor tall, neither fat nor thin.

"You won't win, Alastor," the Deacon spat, as his even voice held a hint of defiance. "We keep the balance."

Alastor laughed, a sound devoid of humor. "There will be no more balance. Tell me where his bones are."

The Deacon clammed up, his lips sealed, he refused to release any information. The location of Lucifer's bones was a secret few were aware of.

Alastor leaned in, whispering the final words the Deacon would hear. "Your hope is a lie. Your fight for balance is meaningless." He shook the Deacon by his shirt. "Lucifer's bones. I need them."

The Deacon shook his head. "No."

The Deacons fell. Alastor slaughtered them one by one. None would release the location of Lucifer's bones. With the Deacons dead and the Safe House reduced to rubble, Alastor surveyed the destruction he had wrought. The fires burned brightly, casting a hellish glow that illuminated his path to the next Safe House. He felt a dark satisfaction knowing he'd eradicated yet another point of defiance against Lucifer's rebirth. He had a greater mission to fulfill, and nothing would stand in his way. Hell would belong to Lucifer once again, and Alastor would rule with an iron fist, crushing any who dared to oppose.

———

There were twelve Deacons in the room reserved for questioning at the Elmira Safe House. Three sat behind a table as though waiting to hand down a sentencing. They were all plain faced, dull, brown hair and brown eyes, they were anyone and everyone. If a Deacon walked down the street not a soul would recognize or remember them. This was the way of the Deacons.

"Forty Safe Houses have been demolished," a Deacon said.

"Survivors?"

"None of us survived. Only survivors are the souls that were there for sorting."

A Deacon seated at the table nodded, thinking.

"The destruction will come to us, we knew it would."

The Deacons all replied in monotone chatter, each with an idea or a plan for survival.

"We leave now. Go into hiding."

"No. We cannot leave the newly dead souls to linger and turn."

"Once they destroy us all none of that will matter."

"We need to hide."

"We need to get out of here."

"We cannot abandon the souls. It will upset the balance."

"There will be no balance on any realm once we are all dead."

The room went silent as the Deacons considered their fate. A world without Deacons was unfathomable.

———

As the days passed, more Safe Houses fell. The Deacons did their duty and processed newly dead souls from the Earthen plane as though nothing were happening.

———

"It's here," Deacon announced.

One grabbed a Newcomer uniform from the supply cabinet. The maroon jumpsuit identified newly dead souls for processing. Or at least it used to, because after today none of that would exist.

Two Deacons grabbed a third by his elbows and directed them toward a supply cabinet.

"Put this on," they demanded. "Hurry."

The building shook with malice as Alastor's army of Demons, dark creatures, and the dead broke down doors and walls. They slammed thru windows and gates, killing every Deacon in sight.

The Deacon who had been pulled into the supply cabinet closed his eyes, feeling the change in the air as brethren were slaughtered under this roof.

"Hurry!" they ripped the white collar off and tore the buttons of the Deacon's shirt. "Change before it's too late."

They moved faster, kicking off shoes and pants and stepping into the Newcomer uniform. It had been ages since the Deacon wore anything besides the black suit and Roman collar. They zipped the Newcomer uniform, stepped into a pair of nondescript white shoes, and mussed their hair.

"You are no longer a Deacon."

The Deacon nodded.

"You have no duty other than to survive."

The Deacon nodded.

"It has been decided." The Deacon giving instructions pointed to the mess hall where detainees were gathering. "Go with them. Abandon everything you've been taught. Survive. Find water. Go to safety and wait."

"What do I wait for?"

They didn't explain; while the Deacons were many, they were also one—one soul that shared debts and prosper, one soul that was bound by a deal with the Crossroads Demon.

The Deacon nodded before being shoved in the direction of the detainees. He stumbled as he filtered between the bodies and became invisible in the crowd. Faces watched him but would never remember him, they could never point him out in a crowd because he looked like everyone and no one.

The other Deacons stayed in the supply cabinet. One collected the uniform, rolled it into a tight ball and hid it behind boxes and bins of cleaning supplies. When they were done, they stepped out into the hall and headed toward the entrance to face their fate. They ignored the Deacon in the Newcomer uniform, knew that they were so nondescript no one would recognize him. He would find safety in obscurity.

The closest body of water was the Nightjar's pond. He could make it there in time. He had to.

———

ALASTOR KILLED every Deacon in the building then left the Safe House with its doors wide open. The nondescript man exited the building at nightfall and ran into the nearby forest.

The Nightjar's pond was a good twenty miles away. As the Deacon ran, he did his best to avoid the dead sleeping in the dark forest. He crushed a leg, tripped over a whole person, fell, and landed with his elbow against a head. It crumpled under his weight and stained his uniform with gore. The Deacon stood and composed himself. The dead slept at night, that was the only good thing, but he had miles to go then the sun would rise and the dead would walk once again. He considered running on the road but decided that would make him too visible. God forbid Alastor noticed him and realized who he was. He shuffled to the side and let his vision adjust to the wavering shadows created by the forest canopy. The ochre Hellsky didn't provide much light, but he could see the bodies lying on the ground now that he took a moment to observe his surroundings.

The Deacon stepped to the side, making his way around the sleeping horde, easy not to step on anyone and damage them further. He still had hope that these souls could be saved and go to their rightful resting place. It wasn't right that they were trapped. These souls didn't deserve to turn and rot here in Hell–not all of them at least.

The Queen had done well to ensure the newly dead made it to a Safe House–better than Lucifer ever had. As a result, the numbers of walking dead had subsided to nearly nothing. Now it was different, now they'd came from the west and filled the forests. Now, if the Deacons ever recovered from this slaughter, they'd have their work cut out for them because there were too many souls. The balance would be tipped further than ever. The Veil between Hell and the Earthen plane just might shred.

Deacon made his way around the sleeping horde and began running again. Twigs snapped and leaves rustled with his movement. He felt the solid ropes of snakes underfoot, the gentle crunch of crushed bugs. Too many creatures had crawled out of the dirt to follow Alastor. He paused every few hundred yards to listen and make sure he wasn't being followed. Deacon ran through the night, while the moon was high in Hellsky until it sank to the horizon. He ran until the Newcomer uniform was torn by branches and bramble, the shoes were stained with dirt, mud, and blood.

He ran until he heard the mournful song of the Nightjar. The creature knew something was happening in the realm of Hell. The ochre sun began to rise.

Moans filled the forest.

The Deacon's heart began to beat rapidly and dread flooded his chest. With the sun rising, so would the dead. They'd follow his noise. They'd follow the snakes and the bugs and the rustling creatures that were after him. He made his way out of the forest, and began running on the road to avoid sounds of snapping sticks and rustling leaves. The deep inhale and exhale of his breaths and the padded footsteps were the only noise for miles.

Only once did Deacon glance over his shoulder to see slithering ropes in the road and scuttling legs. He couldn't control the shiver that sped up his spine and propelled him to run faster than ever.

He ran until he could see the shadow of the Nightjar's

cabin from the road. He paused to catch his breath before jogging down the ditch and into the forest again. He stumbled, landed on low branches with a grunt and snapping of rib bones.

"Dear God," he groaned.

That was all the noise the walking dead needed.

The Deacon heard the guttural groans of the dead, but their footsteps weren't shuffling, no, they were *running*.

Memories of the Fast-Zombie War were easy to come by. It was a tragedy for all involved. The Deacon never thought he'd see something like it again. But the horde he'd stepped around delicately were coming full force now. He could hear their footsteps. They were moving faster than the Deacon ever thought he could.

Running and running and running and...

"Grrr," a rotten toothed man leapt at the Deacon, smashing him to the ground, jabbing broken ribs into his lung.

Teeth snapped. The Deacon struggled; he wasn't trained in combat. His kind hired out force when they needed to. He was weak, muscles burning with the effort it took to keep the snapping jaws from grabbing his skin.

There were more running toward him. Soon he'd be the bottom of the pile, consumed to nothing but toothpicks and gore.

The Deacon twisted to the side, pain searing though his ribcage. He found a moss-covered rock, fingers stretched and clawing to get ahold of it. Fingernails scraped and tore. When he finally gripped the rock, he slammed it into the side of the dead man's head.

It fell away, skull caved in. Ichor dripped.

The Deacon scrambled to his feet, recognized the Nightjar's pond in the distance. He also noticed the dark outlines of the fast dead coming toward him.

He ran; chest heaving, ribcage burning, lung collapsing, and blood filling his mouth. He'd never tasted the sweet tang of his own blood before. He choked on it, stumbled, fell to his knees before finding some strength inside of him to get up.

*Get up. Get up. Get up.* It was the chanting in his head as though every Deacon that ever lived was urging him on. They might all be dead, but they were compelling him to *move.*

He made it to his feet. The fast dead were not far behind–they'd outrun him. Just a few more heartbeats and they'd be gnawing on his spine.

The lights were off in the Nightjar's cabin, and her sad warbling had stopped. He imagined she was watching from the dark windows, hoping for a child sacrifice, and losing interest when all she saw was a slowly dying man.

The Deacon ran like he was running from the law for a crime he did not commit, he ran for freedom, he ran for balance, he ran for hope, he ran for–

He tripped in the slick mud, dropped, rolled and rolled and rolled, broken rib stabbing further into his lung. The pond was there, and wetness touched half of his body. Cool dark water.

*Get up. Get up. Get up.*

He stumbled to his feet and fell face first into the deep water of the Nightjar's pond. The soft current carried him away to safety.

# Six

*Then*

Alastor didn't have wings. Lucifer had made him with a lesser-Demon female, much like Clea. He dropped his seed in the wind and left it to grow without guidance. He was nothing more than an errant weed to his father. Alastor wasn't raised in the castle in the burning caves, no, he was raised in a dirt floored hovel of the mountains. The only thing he had to acknowledge his heritage was the Basilisk tooth blade that was gifted to him and the voice in his head that wouldn't stop. It was incessant. What started as a dream, a desire, now was full blown screaming in the voice of Lucifer, his father, demanding he find Lucifer's bones and revive him.

Alastor couldn't fly, but he could run and drive and hide in the shadows. All of this came in handy as he led the Fast-Zombies back to the castle in the burning caves.

*Find my bones*, the voice in his head demanded.

"I'm trying," Alastor replied, rubbing his temples, wishing the voice would stop. He'd been in the middle of a collection on the Earthen plane when the voice started. Alastor had to leave his second in command in charge of the skin trades. The business was bringing in loads of souls, which he split between himself and the Raven King. Alastor didn't hold a throne in Hell – yet– but he'd regained power with the skin trades. It had taken years to rebuild what Shay and that half-breed Angel had cost him, but he'd gotten there. He'd gotten there and stayed under the radar by paying off Hellions and making promises and slithering in the dark.

Alastor traveled between realms using an illegal portal constructed in the West. During Meg's reign she'd destroyed most of the portals during the Fast-Zombie War and left them demolished, forcing the movement between realms to a trickle. This made the Deacons happy, and others livid.

*Find my bones*, the voice in Alastor's head demanded.

"I'm coming," Alastor promised.

*Kill them all*, the voice insisted.

"I will."

*Kill her*.

Alastor rubbed his face, wishing the voice would stop.

"Promise me you'll stop when it's done," Alastor said. "You'll leave me alone."

The voice was unrelenting and its now silence made him uneasy.

Alastor stood on a cliff ledge of a crumbling highway. The dead from the west were bottlenecked. He took a knife, cut the soft skin of his wrist, and held it out over the horde.

Alastor learned something important from the Fast-Zombie War: if the dead consumed the blood of Archangel royalty, they became *fast*. He figured the same was true for a bastard son of the original fallen Archangel Lucifer. The dead lapped at his blood as it dripped, and it didn't take long for the dead to convert. They became faster, easier to control, especially with the giant Basilisk that followed.

Still covered in rotting gore and dried blood of the baby Basilisks, Alastor didn't look that different from the dead. Didn't smell much different either.

*It was all coming together*, Alastor chuckled to himself. The laughter was awkward and weak because all he wanted was the voice in his head to stop. He even prayed it would stop.

*Find my bones. Find my bones. Find my bones. Find my bones. Find my bones!*

# Seven



*Meg*


*Poof* – I travel to the front stoop of the chapel in the graveyard. For a moment, I enjoy Hellbreeze as it covers my face and bends the reedy grass that has grown up around the safety fence. The chapel in the graveyard is peaceful. It's been a safe place for those I consider close as family. Noah and Nightingale and Thrush have lived here for years. Two ghosts and their son in the only place where they could find peace in the realms, strangely. I think back on my life, to a time when I thought I was simply human on the Earthen plane. The idea of ghosts raising their living child would be absurd, but now it's just another day amongst supernatural beings in the realm of Hell.

There's commotion outside the fence. Bodies shuffling, the whisper of snakes slithering, the chatter of bugs. The castle in the burning caves isn't far from here, and the sound of battle echoes. A chill slides up my spine. I need to get back there.

I knock, wanting to storm in and make my demands known but I can't do that to Noah and Nightingale. Ages ago I promised to do better, to be better, so here I am trying. However, Nightingale should be expecting me since she woke me up not long ago to warn me of the attack.

The door cracks open.

It's Noah, looking at his wrist like he's checking the time, but he doesn't have a watch. "Sun's barely up, woman, you never eat this early."

"We have an emergency," I say.

Noah pauses, hearing the commotion in the distance. "What is it?" His eyes widen with concern.

"Let me in." The idea of telling this truth in the wide open causes a chill to roll up my spine. I don't want anything else hearing this. Noah and Nightingale may be ghosts but they are formidable in their own way, with their own astral magic. But this is something new and I don't want them surprised.

Noah steps back and opens the door further. "You all must leave. Now." I close the door behind me.

"I can't leave you," Noah says.

I hold up a hand, stopping him from saying more. "Today you will. Today you will take your family and go."

"What's happening?" Nightingale walks into the room, dark hair mussed from sleep.

Their son Thrush isn't far behind. He's nearly grown, fifteen now. With dirty blonde hair and blue eyes, he looks just like Noah did in high school. Thankfully there aren't many girls his age down here or there'd be plenty of broken hearts.

I close my eyes and search for the tether that joins my soul to Noah's. My wings feel heavy. My heart like a stone. It all feels so *wrong*.

"Don't, Meg," Noah warns.

"Get out of here," I warn. I reach deep inside, using the power I'd found once to the gather the tether. I cut it for the second time, the final time. If he asks to link our souls again, I won't. Noah deserves more. He's done his duty taking care of me all these years. He deserves freedom in his afterlife.

Thrush is staring. "Make them listen," I warn. "Make them go to save you," I take it a step too far. "You know who this is. He'll string you up and skin you. He'll make you wish you were never born. You saw what he did to the others. You know what he's been doing for years."

Thrush has trained with the Hellions and they've taken him out in the field. After all, Thrush will be required to serve his time as a Hellion when he comes of age. All the children of Archangel lineage do and will. If not, the family will suffer a curse. Memories of Sparrow's tics and Nightingale's antics before their family curse was lifted flash through my mind. None of us will let that happen again.

Thrush's eyes widen. He knows we've been living with a monster in our backyard. He's found the bodies and been on the hunt for the illegal portal with the Hellions. Thrush turns to his parents. "I want to go. Now."

"Rue and Remington?" Noah asks where they are.

If I learned anything from my father, the Archangel

Gabriel, never tell a soul where you hide your people, not even family. I shake my head. "They're safe," is all I reply.

Noah is standing still. Stone still. Deathly still. Unbelievably still. I guess Nightingale didn't warn him. Good to know I'm not the only one who sucks at relationships.

"Go," I say.

There's no movement except in Thrush's bedroom as he gathers his belongings.

"I banish you from the realm of Hell. You are untethered. Go." I point to the sky.

Nightingale touches Noah's arm. "We will be safe in my family's realm."

I turn, not wanting to hear about Sparrow's realm. He promised a truce since Nightingale was living in Hell with me. But once she goes back, I know Sparrow will lift the truce. He nearly killed me once already, with his sister out of my realm, he'll be back with a vengeance. I'm sure Babylon will strike all treaties, even the one about not totally decimating another realm's policing force. The thought sinks in my gut as I consider how shitty things are about to get.

"Goodbye," I say over my shoulder, running for the door because I can't bear to look at them even though it might be the last time. I owe Noah more, a better goodbye, he's been the best friend a girl could have all these years since we were children. He saw me at my lowest; skipped school together, stole cars and went on joyrides together, fed me when my fake-father didn't. No, I can't look at him.

"You don't get to do that," Noah's suddenly standing in front of me, lopsided grin and handsome features. "You don't get to walk away after everything we've been through without a real goodbye." He runs a hand through shaggy blonde hair.

"I don't like touching people," I remind him.

"I don't like seeing you hurting." He opens his arms, and I step into them in an instant. "And I'm not people."

"I'm going to miss you," I say, pressing my face to his chest and swallowing down the sob that's sticking in my throat. "You must protect your family. Nightingale's world is brutal. Those Angels in the Seven Kingdoms of Heaven are assholes. There is nothing nice about them."

Noah squeezes me and I hug him tighter.

"Goodbye," I say, knowing that I am sending them to live with my mortal enemy. Nightingale is Sparrow's sister, the only place she can go in the Seven Kingdom's of Heaven is the Raven King's lands. I'm sending my best friends to my enemy.

"No. It's never goodbye. Wasn't goodbye when you found my newly dead soul down here. Wasn't goodbye when you ran off to college and left me in that Godforsaken town alone. It's never goodbye." Noah is still smiling. He whistles a light trill like a jay.

I smile, nod and whisper, "Never." I whistle back, a little chickadee chirp, because I must. This is what we do, what we inherited from Nightingale and Sparrow, a greeting or goodbye with birdsong is life.

"We'll see you soon. I'll bring the orange soda and fried chicken."

"Thanks. I really miss ice cold Diet Pepsi though." It was my favorite.

"Haven't been able to find that in ages," Noah smiles sadly.

A sob escapes my throat. I'm not sure why, I've never been afraid to run into danger alone. I knew that letting my guard down all these years would make me weak. Make me soft and emotional. I've spent too long holding close the ones I love. My wings feel heavy, my heart cracks. "I gotta go."

"Go get 'em, killer. Remember, Meg, you're north country trash, you burn *hot*." Noah gives me a wide smile, and everything is right in the world for just a moment... *Suddenly we are sixteen and Noah just showed me how to hotwire a Chevy and he's sitting in the passenger side of that car we stole. I'm driving ninety-five miles an hour down State Route 104 headed for Six Flags, high on life and freedom knowing I don't have to spend another night on that dirty mattress on the trailer floor. The music is blaring, and his arm is stretched across the backrest, and I'm wondering how I got the most handsome boy in school to be my best friend...*

Tears prick my eyes. I don't know if I should be insulted or... *Poof* –I leave.

# Eight

*Meg*

I KILLED SEVEN HELLIONS ONCE. Back then I was alone and broken. I can handle one Demon. One will be easy. One will be nothing.

I fly home. I could have just *poofed* the rest of the way there, but I need to see what I'm walking into. It feels good to stretch my wings and feel the Hellbreeze between the mottled feathers.

The doors to the cave are open. Demons and creatures and the dead wander inside. There are dead Hellions on my lands. Other battle at the driveway and the barracks and the empty stables.

I glide to the balcony outside my bedroom. Landing softly, I crouch and listen. Glancing through the glass it looks like the bedroom door is closed.

*Poof.* I go inside. It's silent, probably a trap. *Poof.* I go to the windows outside the infirmary. It's trashed. *Poof.* I go to the ballroom balcony. I grip my blade and it hums to life, ready to slice. It was the only good thing Lucifer gifted me; a blade forged in the fires of Hell that only cuts in my grip. The Hellions have similar blades.

Klaus is here, his white beard coated in blood splatter. I jump down from the balcony railing and kick the door open.

They come running.

Klaus curses. "I had them," he shouts. "Go to safety."

I slash, cutting a kidney-red Demon in half. Bugs crunch under my boots. Klaus raises his blade and cuts down more of the attackers. I make my way toward him, cutting at the snakes that slither across the floor.

"Where are the rest?" I ask.

"The lair," Klaus says.

I hold out my hand and wiggle my fingers until he grips my palm, his giant hand slippery with gore. I wrinkle my nose in disgust.

*Poof* – we land in the Hellion lair. I wipe a slippery palm on my jeans.

Chel is busted up, his wing cut and face bruised. Tukka looks uninjured but it's hard to see blood on his dark red skin. He's wrapping his wrists for support, must be preparing for a lot of hacking away at intruders.

Skeele starts to move toward me. I pause him with the slight rise of my palm. His lips press into a grim line. He probably wants to talk about the children or Noah. He probably wants to ask me if I'm okay. I'm not. But I can't talk about it right now. This is not the time.

Klaus grabs a towel from behind the bar and uses it to clean the blood off his horns.

Clea arrives in a whisp. "They're fast, child," she warns. My mother can only do so much as a ghost, and I'll take the intel over another body fighting alongside us. She's wringing her hands and making the room cold.

"Fast means Archangel blood," I say.

"Babylon truced," Skeele says.

"They deceive." I move toward the wall of weapons and select a pistol and ammo, and another small blade that fits nicely in my belt. "We get the Basilisk and start clearing the castle."

"Noah?" Chel asks.

I shake my head. "He's gone. It's just us." I circle a finger in the air. "No one else but us."

Skeele is watching me, waiting for weakness, waiting to see me crack–because I warned him I would. I warned him I am not as strong as I used to be. I've controlled the wrath that put me in this throne for too long. My children have never seen their true mother, they've never seen my rage. I couldn't disappoint them like that.

Skeele holds out his hand. "We go to the Basilisk together."

The air in the room feels thick, heavy. I've controlled the rage for so long I'm not sure I can remember how to let it flow, how to let it win. It's tamped so far down; a flattened nail head imbedded in wood, difficult to pull out. I put my monster in a box and entombed it in chains.

"This will be our stronghold," Skeele tells the others. There's a door in the back of the room that leads to private quarters and the new recruit barracks. "Meet here if things go awry. You three, gather what's left of the new recruits and the others."

I take Skeele's hand and shiver. He squeezes with urgency. *Poof* – we go to the old office where the Basilisk are kept.

"Shit," Skeele mutters as he slips on a puddle of slime.

The door creaks as bodies shove against it, trying to get inside.

"Come on, babies." I motion to the slithering bodies in the shadows of the ceiling. "We've got a snack for you."

The Basilisk babies grew too big for the castle. We kept two and released the others. One protects Noah and Nightingale's chapel. Two went to Demore's pond. The others went back to the dark waters of the black river in the Adirondacks of Hell.

We slowly brought them back to the castle in the burning caves as Hellion intel worsened.

Eight heads dip down from above, hissing at the door. Sharp, long, dripping teeth ready to chomp peek from their mouths, eager to consume.

Years ago, I was blamed for the Fast-Zombie War, I was blamed for bringing the Basilisk to the Seven Kingdoms of Heaven. If Sparrow sent this War, I have enough grown Basilisk to end all of Heaven and Babylon.

Skeele is bracing the door, waiting for me to send them into action.

"Now," I say.

He opens it and the Basilisk slither out the door, mouths open, eating everything in the hallway, everything that moves that isn't a Hellion or me.

We follow, killing what they miss, crushing bugs under our feet. We make our way through the castle, and room by room the Basilisk eat the Fast-Dead.

We clear the second floor, then the third, leaving a Basilisk at the stairwell to catch anything that comes up. It's going to stay here and guard the dungeon. If those creatures get out we'll have a shit-fest on our hands and I get the feeling we don't need the distraction with what's waiting for us outside.

On the first level we clear the kitchen. I notice the dead have demolished my snack pantry. Twinkies are crushed, brownies half-bitten, two-liter bottles of soda leak onto the floor.

"We'll get more snacks," Skeele says, searching the room.

"It's just utter bullshit," I say. "You know how long Noah worked stocking that stash." I shake my head, and a new anger bubbles up inside me. You don't mess with the Queen of Hell's junk food stash.

It's probably better this way, I don't need the sugar during battle. I sigh and move on.

We make our way to the ballroom, then the infirmary, then we head toward the main entrance, passing the Hellion lair on the way.

I send a Basilisk inside to wait for us. It paces near the door like an anxious dog.

We head toward the giant wooden doors at the end of the hall. They're secured with a large beam that locks into place. The Hellions must've gotten them closed.

The door surges forward like there's a hundred bodies on the other side.

Skeele glances at me. "You should go to safety. I can do this."

"You won't be doing it alone," I say. I grip my blade and

gather the attention of the remaining Basilisk. "Eat every-thing," I instruct. They hiss at the door, ready, so big there's barely enough room for them lined up in the hallway. Skeele stoops down to avoid scraping their bellies with his horns.

I reach for the beam. Skeele is at my side, lifting. The door blasts inward, knocking us onto our asses.

"Blade ready," Skeele shouts.

I want to tell him I fucking know that this isn't my first battle for my life, but the fast dead trample me, stepping on my arms and stomach. I hold in a few screams of pain and roll out of the way. Glancing at Skeele, I see him slicing at legs and necks. He's on his feet already. Damn I'm slow.

A Basilisk hovers over me, protectively, eating every fast-dead that comes for me. I scramble to my feet. These dead are the things of nightmares, moving faster than ever. Just like the time they licked Sparrow's blood off that rock wall on the earthen plane.

Each one I kill, I imagine I'm slicing the Raven King's neck. If their blood weren't rotten, I'd bite them and drain them just like I did to Lucifer and the others. Unfortu-nately, there is no power in drinking from the walking dead, only gut rot. Not that I've tried it; I asked once, for a friend.

Where are all of these dead coming from? This is so much more than the Fast-Zombie War. What have the Deacons been doing?

I think back to the last time I saw one or spoke with one. It's been months, maybe even years. Things were going so well with them not meddling in my life that I lost track.

A woman with ragged clothing and a lopsided face comes running at me. I step forward and cut, her head falls off. Something concerning comes into my line of sight. There's a Basilisk near the dead tree in the courtyard. And it's huge.

"Skeele?" I shout.

"What?" his voice is strained as he fights.

"Who else would have a Basilisk for a pet in Hell?"

"Only you." His voice is closer as he makes his way toward me.

Two of my Basilisk have their heads halfway out the door, catching as many of the fast-dead as they can.

"Oh shit," Skeele says as he notices the Basilisk near the tree. "That's enormous."

The giant Basilisk snaps forward, grabbing one of my Basilisk by the head and eats it. The remaining four squeal in protest at the death of their sibling.

I notice the most concerning scene. Something more so than a ginormous Basilisk slurping at mine like they're angel hair spaghetti. A cluster of the dead, all wearing black, with white Roman collars. The Deacons, they're dead. Too many of them, maybe even all of them. Behind them, it's not the Raven King like I expected.

It's Alastor.

"We should retreat," Skeele suggests.

"No, we must kill them." I can't bite the dead but I can bite Alastor.

# NINE

In the heart of Babylon, where the golden city's splendor melded the Seven Kingdoms of Heaven, stood the Fountain of Eternity–a shimmering pool of iridescent light that served as a portal between realms. As the Archangels left the courthouse, unaware of the secrets hidden beneath the surface, a disturbance rippled through tranquil waters.

Gabriel noticed though. Meg's father was hyperalert to movement while walking through Babylon. He was once the most powerful of all the Archangels, his vote holding the greatest power. He trusted no one in Babylon after they'd imprisoned him and blamed his daughter, Meg, for the Fast-Zombie War when it spilled into the Seven Kingdoms of Heaven.

So when the rest of the cocky and righteous Archangels left their evening meeting with no worries of the dark, Gabriel was the only one to sense the anomaly. His keen eyes narrowed as he approached the fountain, his wings casting a shadow over the sacred waters to shield the activity from onlookers.

With a sense of foreboding, Gabriel reached out and plunged his hand into the fountain, his fingers tingling with the power that pulsed below the surface. Between the shadows cast by his wings, he could see the outline of a maroon jumpsuit. A Newcomer uniform. His heart banged against his ribs as he gripped the cloth and pulled. What he found sent a shock through his very being–a Deacon, half-alive and gasping for breath, struggling against the vortex-like current of the fountain as it threatened to pull him under. Gabriel could not deny the ancient power and aura that enveloped the man. It was much stronger than he'd ever witnessed.

Without hesitation, Gabriel reached in with another hand and pulled the Deacon to safety, his movements swift and decisive as he lifted the man from the fountain and set him on wobbly feet.

The Deacon's eyes fluttered open and he focused on the large Archangel. "Oh, thank God it's you," he coughed out as water and blood dripped from his mouth. "Hide me, please!" the words came out as a strangled gasp.

Gabriel kept his wings open and used his wide robes to shelter the Deacon, half-dragging the man to a Cadillac Escalade parked nearby.

Something was very wrong, and it was nothing like the bullshit story he'd just heard in the courthouse. The balance between realms was shifting, he could feel it.

Gabriel gathered the injured Deacon and set him in the back seat of the Escalade.

"Lay down," Gabriel ordered. "Do not let anyone see you."

The Deacon nodded, water dripping from his clothing and pooling on the leather seats of the vehicle.

Gabriel quietly closed the door and got behind the wheel. He glanced out the window to ensure no one had seen them before driving toward his lands.

"Tell me what happened," Gabriel said. "Why are you dressed like that?"

The Deacon coughed, and between chattering teeth stained with blood he replied, "The others changed my clothing and forced me into general population so I wouldn't be noticed during the attack."

Gabriel watched the man in his rearview mirror, accelerating the vehicle with an urgency to get home quickly.

"Why?" Gabriel asked.

"All the Deacons are dead. I am the last one."

Gabriel couldn't deny the ache in the Deacon's voice. His story would account for the dwindling number of souls that had reached the heavens.

"What about the Safe Houses?" Gabriel asked.

"Burned or abandoned."

Gabriel entered his lands, hit the button on the console to lock the gates and kept driving past the house and the training grounds for his Legion. He drove to a trail in the forest shrouded in shadow. There was a path only identifiable by a few oak trees and moss covered rocks deep under the canopy. Only Gabriel knew of this place, he'd never shown a soul.

Gabriel got out of the vehicle, went to the back door,

and dragged the Deacon out. The man was shivering and pale.

"Can you walk?" Gabriel asked.

The man nodded but stumbled. The Deacon hissed in pain.

Gabriel looked down and noticed the shimmer of blood. "You're injured. I'll carry you."

"Thank you," the Deacon whispered.

Gabriel carried the man through the forest to a hidden door behind a curtain of vines.

"What is this place?" the Deacon asked between labored breaths, ignoring his slowly deflating lung.

"Safety. Not another soul knows about it. You'll be safe here." Gabriel set the Deacon at a table and dragged a chair closer to prop up the man's foot. He began removing the man's shoe and pulled up the pant leg of his uniform.

Red teeth marks stared back.

Gabriel turned quickly to the Deacon, "This must go," he warned. There were already black lines seeping up the Deacon's leg.

The Deacon nodded in agreement. "I must stay alive."

Gabriel gripped the blade at his side, it glowed to life. He used the tip to cut a strip of material off the Deacon's jumpsuit, then tied it tightly above the man's knee.

The Deacon was watching him with wide eyes. Blood dripped from his mouth and nose as he coughed then paled considerably.

Gabriel whispered a prayer before placing his free hand on the Deacon's forehead, unsure if he could outpower the man. But fear and pain won. The Deacon closed his eyes and went unconscious. In one swift movement, Gabriel cut off the man's leg just below the knee.

*Poof* – Gabriel went to Teari.

———

TEARI WAS FOLDING gauze and resetting her workspace after a long day of healing Gabriel's Legion warriors who had minor injuries from sparring and training.

"I need you to come with me," Gabriel boomed.

Teari startled, spilling a container of cotton balls. She didn't like the sound of Gabriel's voice. "Prepare me a little for what I'm about to see," she warned. As Gabriel's personal healer, she'd been dragged into a lot of shit shows.

"An amputation," he replied.

She sucked in a breath. "I'll get my things." Her hands quickly collected gauze and suture strings... she paused, stared at her own hands for a moment, remembering there was a time that she didn't have hands. They'd been cut off during the Fast-Zombie War, but Meg had saved her and made her whole again.

She turned with her bag. Gabriel was holding out his hand. "So we're traveling like that?" she didn't like the way Gabriel could *poof* from place to place. It made her dizzy, but that wasn't terrible, she'd seen others vomit from it.

Gabriel brought her to the secret cave in the forest. Teari knew the inside, but not how to get there. It was the place Gabriel had hidden his people during the Fast-Zombie War.

Teari turned to find a man in a maroon jumpsuit, his left leg cut off at the shin and bleeding all over the floor.

Worse was the blood seeping between his lips and the gasping sound he was making. He smelled like brimstone. She moved quickly, staunching the blood flow. Her hands hovered over the wound, magic stitching together veins and arteries. She sealed the muscle and secured lose tendons and fascia. She removed bits of rotten tissue, recognizing what she was dealing with. She'd felt that rot in her own body before. "How long ago was he bit?" she asked.

Gabriel shrugged. "I'm not sure. I found him less than an hour ago. Cut off the foot then got you. I could wake him up and we can ask the precise time he was bitten..."

"No," Teari was shaking her head, remembering what it felt like after a limb was cut off. "Keep him unconscious for as long as possible." She glanced at his face. He looked like no one and everyone. "Who is he?" she asked.

"A Deacon." Gabriel's reply was flat, serious.

Teari's shoulders sagged. "It's started then." She moved to her feet, lifted the Deacon and laid him on a nearby cot. She needed a moment to right her words. "Where is Meg?"

Gabriel's face was stone. "I don't know."

"You just came from a council meeting in Babylon. They had no information?"

"They only had bullshit to spew. They know nothing. I don't think they know precisely what's going on in Hell."

"Did they see the Deacon?"

"No," Gabriel assured her. "He's the last one. They're all dead. I believe him."

Dread filled Teari. She knew something terrible would be coming to Hell. She didn't want to believe that the time had come.

"Was Sparrow at your council meeting?" Teari asked.

Gabriel sighed and ran a large hand through black hair that went to his shoulders. Bright blue eyes locked on Teari. "I cannot speak of it, you know this."

Teari nodded. "You have family in Hell," she reminded him. "You once desired heirs to your throne."

"Do not fucking remind me of my own aspirations." He stepped closer to Teari and reached out a long arm, flicking her in the forehead. "This is the deepest pile of shit I've ever seen in my life, and I get the feeling we're only seeing a small portion of it."

"You must worry about Rue," Teari said. "You must wonder if she's safe."

Gabriel rubbed his face, thinking.

Teari wanted to say more but she couldn't because very few knew about Remington and who he really was. As far as the other realms were concerned, Meg only gave birth to one child that day. Remington was a shadow heir. Never spoken about, never announced, never discussed. No one knew he existed besides those closest to Meg.

Teari glanced at the sleeping man, ensured his bandaged leg was dry then stepped further away. "He is the last of the Deacons?"

"Yes," Gabriel nodded.

"Can you feel the archaic energy bound within him?" she asked.

Gabriel's lips pressed into a line. He didn't want to admit anything.

"Maybe you are already aware of this but the Deacons have held the balance of power for ages. They have the ability to cross realms and do as they wish to maintain the balance." Teari took a deep breath, afraid of what she was thinking.

"This man is the last, all that power is harnessed within him. He is a walking time bomb. Stronger than anything we've ever met." She pointed at Gabriel. "Stronger than you, than Sparrow. A collection of souls won't make a difference against him. He might even be stronger than... God."

Gabriel rubbed his beard and contemplated the words of his healer. He waved a hand, dismissing her concern, "Well, he's missing half a leg now, so that might change things."

# Ten

*Find my bones. Find my bones. Find my bones. Find my bones. Find my bones...*

The voice echoed in Alastor's head as he watched the Fast-Dead overtake the castle in the burning caves. He smiled when he saw the Queen and her Hellion Commander at the door. She should have an army out here. But, he'd seen the bodies of the other Hellions littering the grounds. Saw them flying down to capture the dead one by one. They were too fast and the Hellions clearly weren't skilled in fighting creatures like this. If they had trained, they were terrible at it. Lucifer would be rolling over in his grave if he could see how far the throne had fallen since his days. Hellions of Lucifer's time would have shredded anything within a five mile radius. The dead and the rest of Alastor's army would have never gotten this close.

The Queen and her Hellion Commander weren't completely alone, they had a handful of Basilisk, but Alastor's was bigger and stronger. He moved closer and the

Basilisk followed, protecting him. The scent of her dead children pooled in his footsteps.

Alastor's Basilisk snapped forward, grabbing another one of Meg's Basilisk and eating it, head first. Then another, then another. Until there was only one.

Meg shouted, tried to run outside and attack Alastor head on. Skeele grabbed her across the middle and dragged her inside, slamming the doors closed.

Alastor moved closer and knocked on the large wooden doors. "Honey, I'm home!" He shouted as a greeting. "I'm home to take my throne! I'm home to free the true King of Hell!"

He motioned to the Basilisk and it began butting the door with its head. Wood cracked, stone crumbled and fell from the walls above. Alastor took a few steps back as his Basilisk destroyed the entrance. The doors snapped and fell inward. The Basilisk slammed against the stone walls until the opening was large enough for it to move inside.

Alastor stepped through the threshold of the castle in the burning caves and it felt like he'd come home. He spread is arms wide and sucked in a deep breath. Ah, woodsmoke and pine and true blood. This was the smell of home. This was the home he never got to visit, never got to live in; it was so much better than the hovel in the mountains.

*Find my bones. Find my bones.* The voice of Lucifer was louder here, pounding in his head until he could barely hear anything else. Lucifer's voice was so loud Alastor didn't hear the shrieking of Meg's Basilisk as it defended the door to the Hellion lair, only to die by one of its own kind.

# Eleven

*Meg*

"It's dead," I say, glancing to the Basilisk slithering against the ceiling.

"There's one at the stairwell, guarding the dungeon," Skeele says.

"That thing will kill it." I pace the lair, rubbing at the small cuts on my arms and smearing the blood inadvertently.

Skeele has a deep cut across his thigh and one on his cheek. I can't stop my mouth from watering at the smell of his blood.

As though Skeele could sense my hunger, he rounds the bar and pulls every bag of blood out of the fridge.

"Eat," he says, ripping open a bag for himself.

He knows better: fresh blood will make us stronger. But we don't have time for that.

I cross the room and start drinking. It quells the hunger

to a dull hum in the background. I glance up and find Skeele watching me. Both of us wish my teeth were biting into his neck.

Something slams against the door to the lair.

Footsteps and shouting come from the hall at the back of the room that leads to the private quarters and barracks. Tukka and Klaus blast through the door with a few of the newer Hellions.

"What's going on out there?" Skeele asks as I drink.

"There's too many. Too fast." Klaus squeezes blood and gore from his beard. It's no longer white but completely stained rusty red.

"Where's Chel?" Skeele asks.

"Gone." Tukka grips his blade, grimacing.

"Brace that door," I say. I glance to the bar, moving to place what's left of the bagged blood in the fridge.

More heavy footsteps echo.

"Wait!" a familiar voice shouts. It's Chel!

Tukka grabs Chel's arms, pulling him inside the room before Klaus slams the door closed. "We thought you'd been killed."

"Ya fucks didn't look too hard for me," Chel grumbled, swiping gore off his arm.

Chel glanced at the bag of blood. Then me. Then the other Hellions.

Simple math. One Queen of Hell with a blood bond to her Hellion Commander, two Hellions that I know well, and three whom I am barely acquainted with. If I learned anything from Jim besides sturdy boots and a good gun–it was prep food for the long haul. There's barely enough bagged blood to make it two days between us all. We'll be starving in about twelve hours. If Alastor lets us live that long.

The Basilisk turns and looks at me.

Damn. Another mouth to feed.

———

There's a knock on the door to the Hellion lair. Skeele moves forward like he's going to answer it.

"Let me." I step in front of him and tip my ear toward the door. Skeele flashes me an irritated look.

"What do you want?" I ask.

There's a chuckle on the other side.

Clea arrives in the room, wringing her hands. "It's another child of Lucifer. A halfling." Clea motions to the side of her face, dragging her hand down it. "He's scarred."

"You never told me I had an uncle," I say, watching Clea.

"I'm sure I have plenty of brethren but I was never formally introduced. Lucifer wasn't the Sunday dinner and family holiday type." Clea glances at the door. "That Demon out there; he's big, powerful. I think it's the one your Hellions have been watching."

"We've known about him for a long time. It's the one who kidnapped Shay." I remind her. "Should have killed him a long time ago. Truthfully, I was expecting someone else to show up today."

"Sparrow?" Clea asks.

"Yes," I say.

"This is a surprise that the Raven King didn't come for you. Does that mean the Seven Kingdoms of Heaven are upholding their truce?" Skeele asks. "Or are they blind to this upheaval?"

I shake my head. "I haven't spoken to any of them."

"Not even Gabriel?" Clea asks, biting her lip.

"Some things are better left avoided," I say.

Hours pass and the threat outside the door remains. Our hunger grows with the passing of time. The bagged blood has been shared but what little remains isn't enough to sustain a Hellion for an entire day, especially a day thick with battle.

The Basilisk shifts anxiously at the ceiling.

There are footsteps at the back door to the lair. Something is coming up the hallway.

The room is thick with tension and a palpable anxiety settles over everyone like a suffocating blanket. Klaus paces back and forth, his footsteps echoing off the walls of the dimly lit lair.

I could hear my own heartbeat, the rhythmic thud in my chest a stark reminder of what was at stake. Chel stands beside me, his usual smirk replaced with lips pressed to a line and stress wrinkles. Skeele and Klaus are positioned strategically around the room, their eyes sharp and focused.

Suddenly, a crash shatters the silence and the door threatens to splinter under the force of the impact.

"Open the door, don't let it break," Skeele says.

Klaus moves closer, hitting the latch.

A crash shatters the silence as the door slams open under the force of the impact. I feel a cold rush of adrenaline as I recognize the dead, the grotesque forms spilling into our holdout.

"Here we go," I mutter under my breath, gripping the weapon in my hand tighter.

The smells hit us first, that rancid stench of decay and death. It was almost overpowering, but I force myself to focus.

Chel is the first to react, moving with a fluid grace that seemed unnatural after a lifetime of Hellion training. His blade slices through the air, connecting with the first zombie's neck, sending its head rolling across the floor.

"Keep them back," Skeele shouts, his voice cutting through the chaos.

One comes running toward me. I swing my weapon, the impact jarring my arms. The creature staggers back but I don't stop. I can't afford to. I kick one in the back, throwing it off balance. Klaus finishes in with a swift strike to the head.

To my left, Skeele is a whirlwind of motion, his blades a blur as he cuts down anything that comes through the door. My Hellions are methodical and precise, each movement they make calculated and deadly.

"That's all of them," Klaus calls out, his voice steady despite the bodies littering the floor.

Someone slams the door closed and we drag the headless bodies to a pile on the far side of the room. I gag a little at the stench.

"Being locked in here with this is not optimal," Klaus says with a groan of disgust.

There is another knock on the main door to the Hellion lair. It turns into a repetitive pounding.

Chel is standing there looking distraught for the first time ever. "We can't do this alone."

"We have each other," I say.

"We need more!" he shouts.

"Stop," Skeele holds up a hand. "We can do this. It's just *one* Demon."

"That thing is more than a simple Demon. We all know it. He's been on our radar for years. We should have killed him when we had the chance at the Black Mansion. Should have chopped him to bits before setting fire to the place. And we should have killed whoever brought him back to life." Chel's eyes land on mine. "I've fought him before. He's stronger."

Chel and Jed battled Alastor long ago to save Shay. Alastor kidnapped her. Jed stabbed him with a Basilisk tooth knife to immobilize him, then Nero set him on fire. It should have ended him, Alastor should be nothing but ash. But *someone* brought him back, with a vengeance.

"We couldn't risk upheaval of the higher Demon caste." Skeele paces. "This was a delicate situation."

No, it was a straightforward one. But I didn't want more death in my realm. It's hard admitting I was wrong, that's why I can't say it out loud.

"Chel, you're going to take the back corridor out of here. Go to the portal, any portal. You might just have to find water. Get to Babylon. Get to Gabriel," I say.

"You'll all die if I leave," Chel argues. "He's too powerful."

I shake my head.

"Do as your Queen instructs," Skeele says.

"You really want to involve Gabriel?" Chel asks, looking concerned. "He hasn't helped. Where is he now?"

"He is bound by the rules of the Seven Kingdoms of

Heaven. If he is not here now, he has good reason. You need to go to him." I hope my words are true. My father has helped me before in Hell. A long time ago he snuck through the Veil to seek vengeance and help rescue me; I'm sure he'd do it again.

Chel rests his hands on his hips and glances at the wall of weapons. He closes his eyes, paces slowly and takes a deep breath, considering my orders. "Fine," he says with a nod. "I'll go."

"Good." I turn toward the door to the Hellion lair as something thuds against it, causing the wood to bend.

The last Basilisk is watching warily.

"You go with Chel," I tell the Basilisk, waiting to see if it understands.

"No, Meg..." Chel's voice is demanding. "I don't need it."

"Then send it back when you've escaped." I try my best not to glance at Skeele, sensing he does not agree with this plan. "You're not doing this alone."

Chel rubs his face. "This is a bad idea."

"We are out of good ideas," I say. There are no good ideas. We must get out of this room. We can't go out the back with Chel; that will cause too much attention. No, Chel is going to run and I'm going to open that door and let the Demon in.

Chel takes a few weapons off the wall, then I give him the last bag of blood.

"No–" he argues.

"Eat it and go." I walk toward the door to the Hellion lair. "Go now."

Chel turns tail and whips open the door at the back of

the lair. The Basilisk goes first, eating whatever dead roam. Chel follows.

"Hide that door," I tell Klaus, motioning to furniture that's big enough to conceal it; a large bookshelf and a bureau with wide doors.

I reach for the door handle of the lair. The door bulges again. I rip it open and face my fate with open arms.

# Twelve

*Meg*

"Ah, Queen Meg, it's about time we formally met." Alastor walks into the lair like he owns it.

His Basilisk slithers in the hall, going still before darting away.

Stones sink in my gut. I hope it's not going after Chel and my last Basilisk.

"What do you want?" I ask.

"I'm looking for something and you just might have it." Alastor wags a finger in my face. "The bones of Lucifer. Where are they?"

My body goes stiff. My mind goes blank. "I don't know."

"Don't play dumb, now." Alastor paces the room, inspecting.

Skeele walks closer to me, like a lion sizing up its prey.

"Uh uh," Alastor warns Skeele. "Step away from her."

The look on Skeele's face is nothing less than murderous. The veins in his arms bulge with rage at Alastor's threatening tone.

"So you don't know where Lucifer's bones are? Tragic." Alastor inspects what remains on the wall of weapons. A few daggers, a nail bat, a few swords.

"I was unconscious for weeks," I say. "I never asked."

"Hm. You should have." Alastor brushes a hand over his dark hair, smoothing it back so he doesn't look so disheveled. The movement revealed melted skin on half of his face. "This is going to be harder than I thought." Alastor selects the nail bat and swings it a few times. "I need those bones." He shivers, his eyes glazing over like he's mentally gone somewhere else for a moment. He blinks and comes back, shaking his head like he's chasing away a bad dream.

Something isn't right. I wonder if he's possessed by something right now.

"We don't have the bones," Skeele says. "Leave us."

Alastor chuckles before skipping a few steps toward the nearest Hellion and slamming the nail bat into his head. Blood splatters and the Hellion drops to the ground, skull crushed.

"I can do this all day," Alastor says with a shuddering of his body. "Feels good, killing things. I've suppressed it for too long."

He points the bat at me. "The bones." Ichor drips from the nails.

"I don't have them," I say, a sickening feeling crawling up my throat.

Skeele inches closer to me. I want to tell him to stop

looking suspicious. I have sharp teeth, I can protect myself. I think. It's been years since I had to draw upon the rage that seated me in the throne of Hell. I think I can do it again.

Alastor wags the bat and black blood drops off the nails, spattering the floor. "Tell me, Queen."

"I can't, I don't know where they are." I keep my chin high, my body still. I have been a very good liar throughout my life, this is no different. No different than all those other lies I spewed.

Alastor points the bat at me, the gore-covered end scraping my arm. A strip of skin breaks open.

"Who would know?" Alastor asks.

I stare, search my thoughts. "The Deacons."

Alastor's face is impassive for a moment before it crinkles in pain, dropping the bat, both hands fly to his ears, covering them. "I need the bones!" he screams like a madman, eyes wide and burning, hair matted to his face. The room goes silent, not a breath echoing on the stone walls; only his tormented voice fills the void as he screams.

# Thirteen

*Find my bones. Find my bones.* The voice of Lucifer was louder than ever. Alastor's scream brought silence, but only for a moment as he could feel the whispers of Lucifer in the back of his brain, threatening to overtake his mind.

Alastor chanted in Hellspeak and the floor opened up. Lesser Demons and strange creatures began crawling out. Cockroaches and spiders and black beetles swarmed the group, biting and scratching, bringing chaos and destruction.

Skeele stepped closer to Meg. Klaus followed. Tukka was too far away to get closer without making a scene.

A knowing look passed between Tukka and Skeele. There was another Hellion with Tukka.

The creatures scrambled toward them, bugs skittering and snakes slithering. Skeele, Klaus, Meg, Tukka, and the remaining Hellion recruit begin slicing at the creatures and stomping them.

Alastor waited, letting his creatures do the hard work.

Slowly picking up the nail-bat, he gripped it and shook away the voice in his head.

The fighters' blades were dripping with ichor, their boots slimy with bug guts. Lesser Demons are thrown against the wall, slapped across the room. They bite. One hung from Klaus's arm, teeth sinking deep as the Hellion roared and tore the creature off, ripping out a good chunk of skin. Klaus gripped the little Demon with two hands and tore it in half, throwing the pieces in defense as more came crawling out of the hole.

The silence that followed was deafening, a stillness that belied the imminent threat. They stood ready, weapons in hand, eyes locked on the gaping hole in the floor that seemed to breathe malevolence.

Meg glanced at Skeele, his eyes gleaming with predatory focus. Klaus stood tall, his stance disciplined, his blade glinting in the dim light. Tukka, ever the wild card had a manic grin on his face, twirling a chain with restless energy.

The ground trembled, a low rumble sending a shiver down Meg's spine.

Tiny Demons and creatures of chaos clawed their way out of the darkness, their eyes glowing with unholy light. They moved with primal ferocity, their growls and roars filling the air, a cacophony of madness and rage.

"Here more come," Klaus muttered, his voice steady but laced with tension.

The first lesser Demon lunged at Klaus, who was closest, a twisted mass of muscle and teeth. Klaus moved instinctively, his blade slicing through the air with a satisfying thwack as it connected with the creature's head, sending it crashing to the ground.

"Stay focused," Skeele said, swinging his blade to keep the next one at bay. "We can't let them overwhelm us!"

Skeele was a blur of motion, blades slashing through the Demons with brutal efficiency. He fought with a focused intensity, each strike fueled by a deep-seated rage. "Just keep them coming," he growled at Alastor, his voice a guttural snarl.

Tukka laughed manically, his chain spinning faster and faster as he waded into the fray. "This is what I've been waiting for!" he shouted, his eyes alight with a wild excitement. "Let's show these bastards what we're made of!"

Klaus was a pillar of strength, his movements precise and controlled. He fought with a calm efficiency, his sword cutting through the chaos with deadly accuracy. "Watch your flanks," he called out, his voice carrying over the din of battle. "Don't let them surround you!"

Meg could feel adrenaline coursing through her veins, sharpening her senses and dulling the pain of each new scratch and bruise. They fought as one, a seamless unit, each covering the other's weaknesses, their movements perfectly synchronized.

The creatures kept coming, a seemingly endless tide of darkness and fury. Tukka lashed out with his chain, feeling the satisfying crunch of bone as it connected with a Demon's skull. "Just keep fighting," he gasped, barely pausing to catch his breath.

Skeele let out a triumphant roar as he tore through a mess of Demons and bugs and snakes. His blade dripped with black blood. Meg glanced to him, just once to make sure he was okay, and his eyes were ablaze with determination.

Meg swung her blade, splitting heads, chopping necks. The scene was all very bloody and gory and disgusting. Alastor was impressed. He didn't know much about Meg, had never seen her in action, but this was a tiny bit impressive. He was slightly disappointed that she was going to die immediately.

"Get back," Skeele warned.

"I'm fine," Meg shouted back, stomping on a giant cockroach. "Everything is fine," she muttered under her breath.

But then it wasn't. Alastor was headed for the duo on the opposite side of the room. Klaus and the other Hellion didn't see him, too busy with battling the creatures. Alastor swung the nail bat at the other Hellion, piercing his shoulder, then his stomach, then the back of his neck. The last hit took him down.

Tukka noticed and raised his chain.

"What will it be, Queen Meg?" Alastor shouted. "Tell me where the bones are or I kill your Hellion."

"You've already killed enough," Meg shouted back.

"What's one more?" Alastor said as he swung the bat toward Tukka.

The Hellion moved fast, swinging his chain blocking the nail-bat before it had a chance to crush his skull.

Tukka and Alastor swung weapons, barely missing each other. Metal slammed against wood. Alastor lurched forward, hitting him in the knee. The Hellion roared as nails pierced his leg and his knee gave out.

A sickening squelch echoed in the room as Alastor pulled the nail-bat out of Tukka's leg.

Tukka let out a breathless laugh, his chain finally still.

"That was one hell of a fight," he said, a note of satisfaction in his voice.

*"Bleed her out. Bleed them out until they confess where my bones are,"* Lucifer's voice shouted in Alastor's mind.

Alastor swung the nail-bat, circling the air until there was enough momentum then he whipped it in Klaus's direction.

Klaus didn't see the nail-bat coming, he was too busy tearing apart lesser Demons and tossing their body parts aside. The nail-bat hit him in the back, embedded in his shoulder blade.

Klaus roared as blood dripped out of his skin. He struggled to bend his arm behind his back and pull it out. When he finally reached the handle, he tugged and the nails tore his skin; blood trickled down his body and pooled at his feet.

Alastor smiled, knowing that the two Hellions would die quickly without blood to heal their injuries. He glanced to the Commander, the one named Skeele. He needed to get that one next. Alastor chanted in Hellspeak. Suddenly the ground beneath Skeele seemed to ripple and a dark, writhing mass of small demons, bugs, and snakes emerged from the cracks in the floor. The deluge ascended upon Skeele with an unholy fervor, their eyes glowing with malevolent intent. Snakes wrapped around his legs, tripping him. Spiders and cockroaches and giant beetles bit him.

Skeele snarled, his claws flashing as he slashed at the oncoming tide. He managed to tear through several of the creatures, but for every one he killed, ten more took its place. The sheer number of them was overwhelming. He felt a sharp pain in his leg as a snake's fangs sank into his flesh, its venom spreading through his veins like wildfire. He stumbled, swatting at the bugs that had crawled up his arms, their bites searing his skin. The small Demons leaped onto him, their claws digging into his flesh, their teeth tearing at him with relentless ferocity.

The creatures swarmed until Skeele was a writhing figure on the floor, not an inch of his skin could be seen.

Meg tried to get to Skeele, kicking and chopping at the creatures. She'd never killed so many spiders or beetles in her life. Still, she could barely see him under the creatures.

Alastor called upon his Basilisk next; the giant creature slithered into the lair and it started toward Tukka.

"No," Meg shouted as she tried to clear Skeele of the deluge of creatures that were consuming him. "Leave them alone." Meg was glaring at Alastor. "Leave them. You want me, take me."

"I want the bones," Alastor said.

"I already told you," Meg was out of breath, panting as she fought and bartered, "I don't know where Lucifer's bones are."

"*She's lying,*" Lucifer roared in Alastor's mind.

The Basilisk darted forward and gobbled Tukka in one bite.

"No!" Meg shouted.

A dark smile quirked Alastor's lip. "You've only got two Hellions, Queen." He shrugged. "Well, what's left of them."

"Stop!" Meg shouted, pleaded. Panic pricked through her limbs as she took in the shit show erupting around her.

Alastor chanted and his creatures receded to the hole in the floor, the Basilisk slithered to a corner and waited.

Meg inhaled a sharp breath as the creatures scattered away from Skeele. His right leg had no skin, chunks of flesh were missing from his body, a hole had been bit in his cheek. Dark eyes flashed open and focused on her. She'd spent enough time with him she could read his face, or what was left of it. He was in agony, nearly eaten alive.

"Commander," Klaus started to say as he dashed across the room to offer help.

The Basilisk darted from the ceiling, consuming Klaus in one bite.

Skeele tried to turn his head, a gasping breath echoed.

"No," Meg whispered, grief flooding her body like a tidal wave, cold and unrelenting. Every piece of her threatened to crack, as if her bones had become fragile glass, splintering under the weight of the moment. Her knees trembled, wanting to give in, to collapse under the crushing sorrow. She stared ahead, unblinking, as reality set it. This couldn't be real. Not him. Not now. It was too early in the fight.

Meg's heart screamed to shatter, to weep, to let the agony consume her–but she couldn't. Not here. Not now. This was not the time to fall apart. She forced herself to breathe, each inhale shallow and ragged, her chest tightening as if bound by iron chains.

Meg bit her lip, the taste of copper filling her mouth, a feeble attempt to keep the flood of emotion from breaking through. She couldn't afford to fall apart–not when danger was watching her from across the room, not when other still relied on her.

But inside, the fracture lines spread.

# Fourteen

*Meg*

Skeele tried, fought with all his might. I knew he would. Skeele always said his duty was to serve the throne. I never thought he'd serve it with his life.

Alastor shoves me and I drop to the ground.

"No," the word falls from my lips like a prayer. I scramble to him. "No. No. No."

"Shh." A broken hand touches my face. "Feed." It's his last word before his chest stops moving and his eyes go glassy.

There's blood everywhere. Bones sticking out of his skin. His wings tattered, torn and broken, wings that once enveloped me in privacy, in trust, in tenderness.

*Feed*. Echoes in my mind. His last wish. His last breath.

I kiss him. His lips feeling cooler than ever. No, I can't feed. I can't take the last of him right now. He deserved so much better than me and I can't take any more from him. I press my lips to his cheek, to his shoulder.

"I'm sorry," I whisper. "I'm sorry I couldn't save you." I should have sent him to the Peabody Library. He would have never gone though. He would have never left me alone.

"Pathetic," Alastor sneers.

I hear bone crunching, don't feel the pain until it's too late as Alastor slams his boot down on my wing, breaking it. I cry out easily, giving in like I never have before. Heavy sobs shudder from my chest and I remember why I was so guarded all those years ago. I remember why I let no one touch me. I remember why I never trusted a soul.

It's all falling down, crumbling to nothing. I didn't start with much to begin with. I only took the throne of Hell because I lost my temper and killed my grandfather Lucifer. But watching everything shatter around me is a real downer.

Now, I am nothing. Just a murderer like John Lewis always said. *You killed her and don't you forget it.* Every terrible memory comes flooding back.

I've killed Skeele. It's my fault in the end. I'll never forget it. Something heavy sinks in my chest and shreds to bits.

# Fifteen

Chel ran full bore down the dark passageways, boots slipping on blood and gore. He was following the Basilisk, the creature slithering fast through the hallways, eating the dead and offering him safety out of the castle in the burning caves.

They turned left, then right before coming to the Hellion barracks. They were on the edge of Meg's lands here, past the sparring grounds and the stables. The Basilisk cleared the room of the dead. No one had survived. The Fast-Zombies were too fast. No Hellions remained here.

"Wait," Chel warned the Basilisk. They watched out the windows to be sure no one was nearby. All bodies were on the ground or re-animated and headed toward the castle. "Okay," Chel nodded, motioning to the door.

The Basilisk nosed the door open and the duo slithered into the nearby forest like shadows.

Chel stuck to the cover of the tree canopy while the Basilisk hovered above the nearby road. They ran as fast as they could toward the portal closest to the castle. It was a good thirty miles away; easy to reach by Jeep, but the trek was another story on foot.

They slowed, coming upon a horde of the dead ambling through the forest. Chel breathed a sigh of relief when he realized they were not fast, but the typical stumbling slow. Still, there were so many of them.

The view of the dead Deacons came to mind. Chel was connecting the dots, the rumors of the past few years, and the intel. If there were this many souls trapped and roaming Hell then the Safe Houses were gone.

Chel ran faster, glancing to the Basilisk as it kept pace. He swerved around the dead, felt dread tickling his shoulders when he realized they'd follow and expose him. He cleared the canopy of Hellforest, ducked under the Basilisk as he crossed the road and made it to the cover of the forest again. They were making good time, but Chel was thinking of the scene he'd left behind; he hoped to Hell everyone was still alive. It was the only way. With all these souls collecting, Babylon would come looking for answers. Chel didn't want to serve another throne, he didn't want to go back to the days of Lucifer.

The sun peaked in Hellsky as the duo kept moving. The portal wasn't far and Chel was sure he could get there alone. He made his way to the road and motioned to the Basilisk.

"Go back to the castle," he told the creature.

———

THE BASILISK SLITHERED HOME, past Hellforest and crumbling roadways. It kept to the shadows, afraid of coming across the giant Basilisk who'd eaten its siblings.

The Basilisk digested as it moved, looking forward to a rest in the cozy office which had become home. It would be alone though, the thought came to the creature. There would be no other Basilisk family waiting for it. The Basilisk trembled, mourning its siblings. But, Meg would be there. Meg would take care of it. And there was Noah the ghost man, he'd still feed the Basilisk. The creature was unaware that Noah had left the realm with his family.

The Basilisk made it to the royal grounds, slithered to the open door of the Hellion barracks and took the tunnel that led to the Hellion lair. It sensed no dead wandering, no Hellions. As it slithered slowly, it came to a stop at the closed door. It nudged, hearing the scraping of furniture. The Basilisk pushed harder until the furniture tipped over.

A hiss echoed through the sliver of an opening. The Basilisk could see into the room. Meg wasn't there. It sniffed. The Hellions were dead.

Sadness overwhelmed the Basilisk as it realized everyone was dead or gone. It began backing up as the threatening hiss of Alastor's giant Basilisk echoed in the emptiness.

It moved away, slithered as quickly as it could out of the hallway, then out of the Hellion barracks, then away from the castle grounds. The Basilisk took to the sky, avoiding the dead and anything else it might come across. It slithered to the only place it knew where to go, the Black river in the Adirondacks of Hell. The Basilisk went home.

# Sixteen

Thrush grabbed the small blade Chel had given him during training and tucked it into the pocket near his belt. He picked up his bag and secured it on his back. There was only time to grab a few things from his room; a few books he'd taken from the castle, clothes, small weapons, and snacks. His parents were pacing the living room when he finally left his bedroom.

Noah glanced at the clock, "We gotta go. It's getting closer."

Nightingale was standing near the door. "Now, son. Quickly and quietly." She opened the door, careful that the hinges didn't squeak. They crossed the lawn and paused near the gate to the high fence that protected their sanctuary in the graveyard. Past the chain link, they saw snakes and bugs and small creatures of havoc headed toward the castle in the burning caves.

Noah mouthed, "Follow me."

Thrush nodded.

The gate opened silently, not drawing attention from the creatures on the ground.

Thrush ran as fast as his legs would carry him, his heart pounding in his chest like a war drum. He glanced at his mother beside him, her face set with grim determination. Since his parents were technically dead, they could flash where ever they wanted, but they stayed by his side. Thrush was grateful for it. They had their limitations being spectral beings and all, but they did their best. They still functioned as though they were very much alive.

"Stay close, Thrush!" Noah called out, his voice strained but firm.

Noah glanced back and Thrush could see the worry etched on his father's face. Nightingale's eyes darted around, scanning the Hellforest for any signs of movement. Escaping during the day hours meant the dead would be wandering.

The castle in the burning caves loomed to their right, a sinister silhouette against the ochre Hellsky. The cries of Demons echoed through the air, growing closer. And... there was another sound...

"No," Noah muttered, slowing to run by Thrush's side. He pointed to one of the dead. It wasn't ambling around looking lost like they usually were, this one was running toward the castle.

"Fast-dead," Nightingale warned. "Stay clear of them."

They ran faster, further.

"We are almost there," Nightingale said, her voice a mix of hope and desperation. "The portal is just ahead."

Thrush's legs burned with fatigue, but he pushed himself harder. He'd trained hard for this day. The portal was their only chance. It shimmered faintly in the distance, a beacon of hope in the darkness. But as they drew closer, he saw the dark shapes moving around it.

"Demons," Thrush said just loud enough for his parents to hear, pointing toward the portal.

Noah's jaw tightened. "We have to get through them. There's no other way."

The three skidded to a halt, hiding behind a jagged outcropping of rocks. Thrush peered around the edge, counting the Demons. There were five of them, grotesque creatures with leathery wings and claws that gleamed in the hellish light.

"We need a distraction," Nightingale whispered, her eyes narrowing as she formulated a plan.

Thrush's mind raced. He looked down and spotted a loose, heavy rock. It wasn't much, but it might just buy them the time they needed.

"I'll throw this," Thrush said, hefting the rock. "When they go to check, we make a run for it."

Noah nodded. "On my signal."

Thrush took a deep breath, trying to steady his trembling hands. He waited for his father's signal, the tension stretching out every second into an eternity.

"Now!" Noah hissed.

Thrush hurled the rock with all his might, watching as it arced through the air and crashed into a distant pile of debris. The Demons' heads snapped toward the noise. They moved to investigate.

"Go!" Noah urged, and they sprinted from their hiding place, making a beeline for the portal.

The Demons saw them and let out enraged roars as they ran back toward the portal.

Thrush's heart pounded harder, adrenaline coursing through his veins. The portal shimmered tantalizingly close, but the Demons were closing in fast.

Nightingale reached the portal first, her hand outstretched toward the shimmering surface. "Thrush, hurry!"

Thrush pushed himself harder, his feet barely touching the ground as he raced toward safety. Noah was right behind him, glancing back to see the Demons almost upon them.

"No!" Nightingale shouted. She waved for Thrush to run around the portal. "The fast-dead are coming."

"Change of plans," Noah said, grabbing Thrush by his shirt.

The fast dead didn't pick favorites, they went after whatever moved, whatever was closest, and the Demons had their attention.

"Keep running," Nightingale said, waving, "this way."

Thrush lunged with a final burst of speed following Nightingale as she changed course.

"Where?" Thrush asked between heavy breaths.

"The pond is the closest." Noah was running by Thrush's side.

The sounds of hundreds of feet running echoed through Hellforest. Thrush glanced from side to side, didn't notice the branches on the ground and tripped.

Noah was lifting him to his feet harshly. "Keep going," he urged.

Thrush limped for a few steps before swallowing down the pain in his ankle and resuming his previous speed.

"It's not far," Nightingale said.

Thrush knew better; it was a good distance away and he wasn't sure he could keep running at this pace, but he'd try his hardest. They ran across empty roads and through forests littered with wandering dead.

Nightingale finally slowed near a shallow stream. "It's up here." She motioned toward the dark pond in the distance. "We're safe, Thrush. It's not much further."

Noah placed a hand on Thrush's shoulder, his expression a mix of pride and exhaustion. "You did it, son. We're out of here."

Thrush allowed himself a small, weary smile. They had almost escaped Hell but he knew their journey was far from over. There were still dangers ahead, still battles to be fought–

A fast-dead was running toward Thrush. He acted quick, not ready for the speed at which the fast-dead ran. His parents didn't notice in time. Thrush gripped his knife and slammed it into the skull of the fast-dead as it knocked him over.

Thrush groaned, trying to shove the zombie off him but it was the corpse of a rather large man.

"No!" Nightingale shouted, grabbing at the zombie, and trying to get it off Thrush.

"It's dead," Noah said, dragging Thrush out from under the corpse.

Gore and blood stained Thrush's clothing. He shuddered, thankful for his training with the Hellions the past few years. He wiped his knife on his pant leg and secured it again. "Let's go," he said, making a beeline for the pond.

"The Basilisk," Nightingale warned. "There's two."

Noah pointed to the still surface of the pond. "They're not here."

"Go," Nightingale urged.

The trio ran for the pond.

Thrush dove under, a cold sensation washing over him as the soft current pulled them away.

# Seventeen

*Meg*

Alastor drags me to the dungeon. Broken, bleeding. I can't *poof* and travel, my injuries making me too weak. I need blood. I catch a glimpse of my Basilisk that was guarding the stairs. It's dead and dark creatures are eating its flesh. Something worse than dread floods me.

"Plenty of unseen creatures down here," Alastor says as he drags me. "Things I haven't seen in ages."

My broken wing twists and rolls against the stone floor as he drags me through the dark, labyrinthine corridors of the infernal palace dungeon. The only light came from flickering torches casting eerie shadows on the stone walls. The air was thick with the scent of brimstone and tormented wails.

I haven't been in the dungeons in years, never felt the need to. Seems I'm about to become closely acquainted with the creatures that snarl and hiss from behind solid doors. Sharp talons scrape against the stone floor. The creatures howl and screech and pound on their doors sensing the Queen of Hell in their presence. Or maybe it's the Demon dragging me like a sack of shit. A door slams and Alastor wrenches my leg, dragging me into a cell. I should fight. I should try to stand. I should drain every last drop of blood in his body. Confusion and grief bombard me. There's a sickening feeling in my chest, a lurching in my stomach when I smell the rotten blood dried to the floor.

I should stay regal even like this, I should struggle against Alastor as he grips my wrists and wraps rusted chains around them.

Alastor kicks me. "Tell me where the bones are," he shouts, his voice echoing off the stone walls. He kicks me again, stomping on my broken wing. I cry out. The creatures detained down here howl and heckle, excited for their potential release with the changing of the crown.

The room turns cold.

"Child," the voice of Clea echoes in the room. "You must fight him," she begs, dropping to her knees to face me. "Get up. You must get up."

"Get the fuck out of here," Alastor shouts, grabbing a rusted iron rod from the floor and whipping it at Clea. Her wavering image disappears.

"You're a bastard," I say. "She didn't do anything to you." I don't like it when people threaten my mother. She might be dead, but she didn't deserve what was done to her. A rage swells inside me. A long time ago, Lucifer sparked my rage by being cruel to my mother.

"You dare lay hands on me," I hiss, my voice a mix of fury and command.

Alastor's lips curl into a cruel smile. "The days of your rule are over, my dear. It's time for a new order in Hell." His voice is a low growl, dripping with venom.

I fight against the chains, ignoring the sharp pain in my ribs and broken wing. It's too late. Clea needed to give me that pep talk about fifteen minutes ago.

Alastor chuckles with his newfound sense of power, the iron doors of the cell screeching in protest as he closes them.

"You will pay for this treachery, Alastor. Hell will not bend to your will so easily."

"You overestimate your influence, Queen," Alastor sneers, watching me through the barred window in the door.

I am left with the icy chill of the cell, the musky air from damp walls. There is no window to the outside, only a few slivers of light shining past the door. There is something rust colored dried on the floor. Memories surface: this was Sparrow's cell when he was bitten. That's his dried blood on the stones. Ironic.

———

THE AIR GROWS COLDER, the darkness more oppressive. Clea arrives again in wisps.

"No," she mutters as she takes in the scene. "No this can't be happening."

Tears dry on my cheeks as I struggle to get to my feet.

"Can you break these chains?" I ask.

Clea is shaking her head. "Not the iron." She reaches forward but her hands hover over the chains surrounding my wrists. "The iron will just send me to the Astral plane."

"Damn." I jerk the chains and find where they are secured against the wall. The room is barely more than a stone box, dank and reeking of despair. The chains are secured to a metal ring on the wall.

Something shifts in the air, the castle creaks, the prisoners howl louder then go stunned silence. If there were a Hellion here, they'd no longer intervene. The power dynamic has shifted, the unthinkable has come to pass: the Queen of Hell is now a prisoner.

# Eighteen

Nero whinnied and nodded toward the back hallway of the Peabody Library. There was a long, underground hallway that exited near the Patapsco River. An empty plot with overgrown shrubbery and abandoned buildings, Jed had been warding the area for years, doing his best to provide an outdoor living space where Nero could roam freely for a few hours a day. He typically went out at night, when the chances of being seen were low and he could no longer suppress the urge to run.

Nero glanced at the two teenagers lounging in overstuffed high back chairs, reading. They weren't supposed to leave the building, but Nero needed to go out. He didn't use toilets and he couldn't very well leave a pile of horseshit in the hallway. Jed would never forgive him.

Shay and Jed had gone to get food and the supplies needed for housing the kids. They'd promised to be back soon but it had been hours. Nero didn't want to let the children out of his sight. The fresh air might do them some good, he figured. It wasn't healthy for any creature to be locked indoors for days and weeks at a time.

———

Under the silvery glow of the moonlight, Nero led Rue and Remington through the quiet corridor and riverfront surrounding the Peabody Library. The night air was cool and crisp, carrying with it the faint scent of earth.

As they walked, Rue and Remington clung close to Nero. They spoke in hushed tones, their voices a mixture of excitement and longing.

"I miss mother," Rue whispered, her voice tinged with sadness. "I miss Thrush too. I wish they were here with us."

Remington nodded in agreement, his expression mirroring his sister's melancholy. "Me too," he replied softly. "But we have to stay here where it's safe."

Rue frowned, her brow furrowing with confusion. "I think she was wrong, separating everyone. We should be fighting together. We could help her."

Remington chuckled before saying, "Not you, you're too small."

Rue gave him a dirty look. She was tired of everyone protecting her. She'd spent years watching Remington and Thrush train with the Hellions and the most she got was self-defense and knife wielding. She could do more, she just knew it.

Nero paused from nibbling the dry grass near the riverbank and nudged Rue with his snout. He didn't know how to comfort the children, but he knew the dangers of Hell firsthand. He wished he could tell the children something, anything... All he could offer was a soft whinny of comfort.

Rue and Remington exchanged a knowing glance. They looked up at Nero, a sense of trust and reassurance filling them. Rue reached out and pet Nero's neck and that urge to return home which had flared inside her dampened.

"Shay said there are a lot of kids on the Earthen plane. Plenty our age." Remington rose up on his toes to get a good look across the river.

"More than three is a good number of kids," Rue said, wandering away from Nero.

Could you imagine seeing a whole bunch of kids our age every day?"

Remington made a sound that didn't convey excitement. "You've heard mother's stories." His hands gripped the metal railing and he leaned forward, looking into the dark river. "Kids on the Earthen plane are not all they're cracked up to be."

"They could be nice," Rue said.

"They could suck." Remington turned and leaned his back against the railing, his heels stepping just outside of the markings Jed had made on the cement curbing.

A strange noise came from the murky water.

"What was that?" Rue asked, moving closer to her brother.

Nero whinnied a warning and walked closer, trying to nudge the children away from the edge of the protective runes and markings on the ground.

Rue and Remington together, both with a half a foot outside the runes of protection, lit the skies above with a silvery ethereal light like nothing ever seen before. Two rays blasted to the sky and illuminated the night clouds. Every illegal creature that didn't belong on the Earthen plane saw it.

Without the Deacons to keep the balance, creatures slid between the Veils separating realms. Good and bad, dark and light, they all seeped to the Earthen plane, drawn by forbidden fruit. A tempting aura that begged for inspection, a light that hadn't been seen in eons, curious creatures and those looking to slay the unknown, those looking to consume, made their way toward the river.

———

JED AND SHAY returned to the library only to find it empty. They juggled bags filled with clothing, food, and supplies, twice as much as they usually brought home. Shay wasn't sure it was enough. They'd have to go back out again soon. These kids ate a lot, especially the boy. Jed kicked the door closed and enhanced the spell of protection before turning to face Shay. Concern wrinkled her brow.

"Rue?" Shay called. "Remington?" No one replied. "Nero?" There was nothing. Silence. The library was empty.

"I told you it wasn't a good idea to leave a horse in charge of two teenagers," Jed muttered.

Shay felt a nudge down the tether that linked her to Nero. "They're outside," Shay said, dropping her bags and springing toward the back corridor. "Something is happening." Shay's eyes went wide and she shoved blowtorch blue hair out of her face. "Nero is worried."

"Shit," Jed echoed and followed.

Footsteps boomed as they ran hard and as fast as they could.

"Why would they go outside?" Jed muttered between breaths.

"They're kids," Shay said as she shoved open the door.

"No!" Jed pushed Shay aside and sprinted ahead of her, toward the riverbank walkway. "Stay back!"

The runes and spells that Jed and Shay had been working on for years were meant to shield the outside world from the secrets that the Peabody Library and surrounding empty lot held, but it did nothing to shield those inside from what they could see beyond the wards. Jed's gut punched, he'd never seen so many Demons in all his life. A familiar panic surfaced, one reminding him to run and hide and stay alive. He couldn't do that anymore. Too many relied on him.

Nero whinnied, grabbed Rue's shirt with his teeth and tugged her away from the edge of the riverbank. Rue was smaller and easier to move, Remington was going to be harder, the boy was twice his sister's size, lean and built like a warrior.

"Get away from the river!" Jed shouted as he ran toward them, arms waving.

Creatures big and small had collected along the edge of the property. Strange Demons Jed had never seen before lingered, inspecting, trying to get a glimpse of what had sparked the light. The scene was like a cake drawing children to the table. The Patapsco River had become a cesspool of Hellspawn.

Jed's heart thumped against his ribs as he recognized the cloud-like Demon who'd killed his friend Declan. There were more creatures, things with teeth and feathers and tails. But the worst was the Angel hovering in the shadows, squinting, blade drawn, wings exposed.

Shay saw it and panic burned through her body.

Nero saw it and shoved Rue to the ground. He raced forward and grabbed at Remington by the sleeve.

The boy laughed and pushed Nero away. "Stop it," he said, unaware of the danger lurking behind him.

Nero's eyes went wide as Remington leaned back, breaching the wards again.

The Angel's head snapped toward the light and it began to move closer.

Jed saw the light the boy emitted and every warning from his mother, every battle he fought as a child, every dark cloud he ran from came flooding back, a tsunami of will to fight and survive.

"Get away from the river!" Jed shouted, hands out, magic pouring from his fingertips. He shouted words to knit the wards back together and strengthen them, his words sounded like thunder cracking and ocean waves splitting on rock.

Nero reared up, shocking Remington. The boy leaned back again, anticipating getting kicked.

A hand from outside the runes reached for the top of Remington's head. Drawn by the delightful energy of the Shadow Heir. Creatures from all realms loved something forbidden, they loved something unknown, they loved something consumable that they could exploit. They might not have belonged on the Earthen plane but the boy emitting the light belonged even less. Without the Deacons, the Veil was ready to fracture, chaos was about to win.

Nero threatened to turn into the monster. It had been a long time since he'd released fire of vengeance from his throat. He was ready and eager to create ash if needed. He'd burn them all. He'd burn that Angel to a cinder if it reached for Remington's head one more time.

"Don't Nero!" Shay shouted, sensing the change. She didn't know what Nero changing inside the wards would do to him... or her. Worse, she feared he'd breathe fire and burn the wards away and then they'd be completely exposed to the creatures and people of the city.

Nero lurched forward, grabbed Remington's arm between his teeth, the bite sunk into skin drawing blood. He tore Remington away from the edge of the property and inside the wards, dragging him halfway to the door that led inside before finally releasing him.

The creatures moved closer. All of them. They pressed their faces against the protective layer created by the wards like shoppers pressing their noses against a store window. Eager, interested, and ready to *take*. It was a frightful scene; so many dark creatures in one place, hunting the same prey.

Rue backstepped and knocked into Shay.

Shay grabbed onto the girl and ran to the door. Jed went to work, fixing the wards. Nero headbutted Remington. The boy turned and shock slammed across his face as he saw the mountains of Demons searching for what had created the light. Nero whinnied darkly and nodded to the side. Remington followed his gaze and saw the Angel, searching, his face scrunched like he was looking through a waterfall and couldn't focus.

"Inside!" Jed shouted as he backed away from the

warded lot. He grabbed Remington's arm and took off running.

Nero galloped after them.

Everyone clamored inside the door. Jed closed it gently, trying not to draw the creatures to the noise, then he locked the door with heavy chains and strengthened the wards. Jed took a Sharpie out of his pocket, drew new runes, and considered sealing the door completely.

———

"THAT WAS the worst idea in the history of ideas," Jed said, leading everyone back to the main lounge in the library.

"It was the horse's fault," Rue said.

Everyone glanced to Nero and he hung his head ashamed. Nero lowered his eyes to the floor before gazing back up at Shay like a hurt puppy.

Shay reached out and patted Nero.

Jed was muttering something under his breath as he strode to a bookshelf and pulled off a box.

Shay's gut clenched. She knew what he'd planned to do before he even said a word.

Jed grabbed Remington's arm and dragged him over to a table. "You've seen your mother's tattoos?" Jed asked, sweat dripped down the side of his face and he was breathing rapidly.

"Yes," Remington nodded.

"You see these?" Jed held out his arms and ripped off his shirt. He pointed to a marking on his chest, "This protects me from Demons." Pointed to another, "This protects me from Angels. And this," he chuckled as though it was absurd because Jed thought his blue aura was bright but it was nothing compared to this kid's, "this one dims my aura." His finger pointed to a black rune tattooed at the base of his throat. "You can never be too careful."

He paused to open his tattoo case and chose a greenish-black pot of ink. "Take off your shirt," he ordered the boy.

"I don't have an aura," Remington said.

Jed laughed out loud. "Oh, you sure do, boy. And we must hide it if you're going to stay in seclusion on the Earthen plane because that was bright as fuck." Jed was high on magic and this discovery as he assembled his tattoo gun and set up. "Do you have an aura like that, Rue?" he shouted across the room absently before shaking his head in disbelief.

Nero whinnied in response, he'd seen Rue's light but pulled her away before Jed and Shay came running out the back door of the library.

"Wait," Shay warned, "shouldn't we ask Meg?"

"You want permission?" Jed asked. The words came out rougher than he wanted to speak to her but he couldn't help it. Adrenaline was coursing through his veins and it was a high he hadn't enjoyed in a long time. "You want consent? We haven't heard from Meg in weeks. Who knows how deep of a shit pile she's in. This can't wait. We're doing this tonight."

Rue's chin trembled as she watched.

Shay pulled her closer. "He doesn't mean that. We don't know where she is."

Jed was shaking his head as metal clicked. "Sit," he told Remington.

The boy plopped down in a chair then pulled his shirt off.

"Christ," Jed muttered. "Aren't you like fifteen?"

"I'll be fourteen soon," Remington said.

"What have they been feeding you down there in Hell? Last time I saw you, you were this big." Jed held his hand level with the floor and to his shoulder. "It wasn't that long ago."

Remington shrugged. "My dad said it was a growth spurt."

"It must've been something." Jed flicked the button on his tattoo gun and it buzzed to life. "I said I'd never tattoo a kid…" Jed shook his head, felt like he'd been doing that a lot the past hour.

"What if she's dead?" Rue asked.

"No." Shay was shaking her head, trying to shake out the thoughts she'd been struggling with for weeks, but she wouldn't let the girl know. "There is no way she's dead, Rue. Give her time."

"I'm afraid. What if she's afraid right now?" Rue asked. "What if our mom is somewhere alone and afraid and hurt?"

Shay gripped her shoulders. "Your mother is never afraid. *They* should fear your mother." She searched the girl's eyes for understanding. "She is something to fear. Not the other way around."

The noise of Jed's electric tattoo gun echoed through the corridors of the library.

Remington hissed as the needle penetrated and inked his skin.

"You want a spell for the discomfort?" Jed asked Remington.

The boy hesitated before saying, "It doesn't hurt."

Rue focused on Shay, an unspoken question in her eyes.

"Yes," Shay said, exhaling a breath of knowing. "Yes, you're next." Shay was nodding, doing her best to soothe the girl. "You can do this. Jed is right. We need to protect you both." Shay held out her arm to show Rue her tattoos.

Jed decorated Remington's skin with three runes before stopping. One for the aura, one for protection, and the last for strength.

"Come now, Rue," Jed called as he cleaned his machine and retrieved new pots of ink.

Remington went to sit on the dark green couch near the fireplace. Nero joined him, sniffing at the boy's hair and nipping his shoulder in an attempt to comfort him. Nero knelt and curled up next to the couch.

Remington held out a hand and pet Nero between the ears. "Thanks for getting us in trouble, horse," he muttered.

Jed sighed as Rue sat in the chair. "You have to take off the shirt."

Shay started to say something but Rue interrupted her, "It's okay. I have a bra on."

Jed raised his palm and whispered words that sounded like the soft petals of a rose rubbing together in a summer storm. A coolness coated Rue's skin.

"What was that?" Rue asked.

"For the discomfort of the needle," Jed said as he scooted closer. "I must touch your chest and your bare skin." He pressed his lips into a line and glanced at Shay, unsure of how a teenage girl would feel about his hands and forearms leaning on her body.

"It's okay," Rue said. "You forget, I grew up in Hell."

"Your mother kept you close to her. As she should have," Jed said.

"That doesn't mean I didn't see things. I watched movies. I hung around Hellions." She straightened her back. "I know you're only touching me to tattoo the runes." She tipped her chin up. "Just do it."

Jed nodded and scooted closer. Shay sat opposite Rue and watched the girl in case she changed her mind.

Jed inked Rue's skin with three runes; one to dull her aura, one for protection, and the last for strength. Because of her small size and gender, he doubled the rune for strength.

Jed clicked off his tattoo gun and pushed his chair away from the girl. "Go to bed, both of you," he said to the children.

"But... we haven't eaten dinner," Remington said from the couch.

"And you won't. Maybe that will be a reminder to never go outside alone again." Jed slammed the cover of his tattoo kit.

"We went with Nero," Rue said, eyes large and face pale.

"That doesn't count–" Jed started to say but a loud nicker interrupted him. "You go to bed too." Jed pointed at Nero then arced his arm toward the hallway that led to the bedrooms. "Go."

The boy, the girl, and the horse all stood and walked away, heads down and shoulders slumped. After hearing the doors close—Nero's slammed especially loud—Jed turned to Shay.

"What the fuck," Jed said.

Shay moved to him. "Of all the time we've spent with those two children, I have never seen an aura like that come from them."

Jed ran his hand through messy hair then searched his pocket for a tie. "It must be this plane. That's all I can think." He rubbed his mouth and glanced to the corridors of books. "We'll have to research it."

Jed and Shay had spent plenty of time visiting Hell over the years. After everything they'd been through, Meg was like family and even though she was the Queen of Hell, she still insisted on weekend family dinners and holidays together. Of the few Jed and Shay had missed, Meg had shown up and guilted them into never wanting to miss another. Deep down, Jed and Shay knew that the time together was important, it was normal, it was... human.

"They should have eaten before bed," Shay said, looking toward the dark hallway.

"They'll get over it." Jed was tucking his box away on the shelf.

Shay moved closer, reached up on her toes and wrapped her arms around his neck. "When I saw you running out there, magic streaming from your fingers," she inhaled the scent of him and a quiver hit her center, "it was really hot."

Jed chuckled and tugged her closer. "Oh yeah." He kissed her mouth, then her jaw, then the soft skin of her neck.

"You smell like magic." Shay sucked in a breath as he nipped her shoulder. "I like it."

"I didn't realize it had a smell." His hands gripped her backside and lifted her.

Shay's legs wrapped around his waist and blue hair fell over her shoulders as she leaned into him. "I like it when you go all combat mode."

"I could say the same about you, but I never get to see it." Jed's eyes darkened as he watched her.

Shay giggled. "Maybe Nero could take a picture for you."

Jed carried her behind the bookshelves to a private corner. He pressed her back against the shelves and ground his hips against her center.

Shay's blood heated and she tugged at her shirt, tossing it aside. Jed's mouth lowered to her neck and chest as he pressed open-mouthed kisses to her heated skin.

"You didn't have to jump in there and take over," Shay said. "I could have done it."

"You promised to watch over those children," Jed said. "I will not let you fail. I will not let you do this alone." He kissed her harder.

# Nineteen

*Meg*

Alastor steps inside the dungeon, closing the heavy door behind him. He grabs the iron rod from the floor and grips it, testing its weight.

I watch him with half-lidded eyes and try to give myself a pep-talk. *I am Meg, Queen of Hell, Granddaughter of Lucifer, Daughter of the Archangel Gabriel.* My chest still feels empty. Hollow. I think I am nothing and I cannot hide it from myself.

Alastor pokes me in the stomach with the iron rod. I roll away and move to my knees, ready to stand. The chains rattle and go taut.

"What do you want?" I ask.

Alastor smiles and for a moment I am shocked by how handsome he could be if he weren't my uncle and trying to kill me. His eyes flash red. I shake my head and draw on that empty feeling in my center.

"Just tell me where the bones are," Alastor says, jiggling the rod.

I shake my head. "No clue, buddy." I shrug and do my best to look like an innocent, misunderstood girl.

He steps closer, just close enough for me to make the first move. I'm hoping to surprise him with my strength, instead I surprise myself with my lack of. I'm slow. Weaker than ever. I scrape my nails across his skin. Alastor dodges my attacks with ease, his movements fluid and practiced. He grabs my wrist, twisting it, forcing me to my knees. With a swift motion, he drags me against the wall, wrapping the chains tighter.

I pull against them, my skin tearing and bleeding.

Alastor admires his work. "Comfortable?" he taunts, eyes glinting with sadistic pleasure.

I spit at him; there's no other way to communicate my hatred. "You may have me in chains but you will never break me."

He leans in close, his face inches from mine. "We'll see about that," he whispers, hot breath against my skin, eyes black as night. "Welcome to your new kingdom, Queen. Get used to it."

He clears his throat before turning away and wandering the cell. "Now, about the bones."

"I don't know where they are. I told you." I exhale a breath as the chains sag.

He tests the balance of the rod. "Did Clea tell you about me?" he asks.

My gaze roams his face, focusing on the shadows that seem to swirl and move under his eyes and the hollows of his cheeks.

"Have you been wondering where she went?" he asks.

I say nothing.

"Banishing something like her wasn't terribly difficult. Lucifer told me where her bones were." He sighs as though banishing my mother from her home was a boring task.

If I could burn him to ash with my eyes I would. My steady breaths echo in the dungeon as the faint, distant screams of the damned seep in from the open door.

Alastor swings the rod a few times, testing its weight again and his swing arc, lining up the strike.

My stomach clenches, anticipating. I've been hit with random objects before, and I wonder if Alastor knows anything about my upbringing on the Earthen plane. I wonder if he knew John Lewis or Jim? He seems the type, they probably bullied kids in high school together.

He pauses, his head tips to the side. "Tell me where Lucifer's bones are."

"I can't," I say.

"I don't believe you." Alastor swings the iron bar like a batter at the plate, the end of it barely an inch from my nose.

I don't flinch. I prepared for this for twenty-five years. I spent more time as a punching bag for John Lewis and Jim than I have spent as a Queen. It's a training that is hard to break. I'll never forget how to still my body, how to loosen my muscles so the ache doesn't linger afterwards, how to tense my abdomen but nothing else. I've already died once—maybe even twice—nothing Alastor could do to me would compare to that heartbreak. Not sure I ever really recovered from Sparrow's deception.

Alastor snorts and wanders. "I can do this all day. All night."

"You must be bored," I mutter. "Lucifer will use you just like he used my mother. Did he tell you why I killed him? He sent the Basilisk after her. He'll do the same to you. He'll kill you once he's used you up." My stomach growls.

"Oh," one dark brow rises in interest. "You hungry, girl?"

"No," I lie.

"That sounded like hunger. You want some blood?" his smile is sinister and now I can see the resemblance to Lucifer in his features.

I close my eyes, focusing on the remaining flicker of strength. A tiny flame in my center threatened to extinguish.

I lurch forward, teeth bared, ready to bite. The chains snap taut: he's just out of my reach.

"Ah, you are hungry."

"Nope," I lie. "I'm never hungry." My stomach clenches, I'm so hungry I could eat five pizzas or five guys. "I just want you dead."

"Where are Lucifer's bones?" Alastor asks. "Tell me and I'll set you free."

"The Deacons took them." I shudder. "I wanted to burn them but I was overruled." It's a partial lie.

"I need the bones to make the voice stop!" Alastor's eyes are wild. "Tell me where they are!"

"Go ask the Deacons," I shout back. "Oh wait, you killed them all didn't you? Dumb ass!"

He swings the iron rod, hitting me in the ribs. I hiss. "You fuck."

"That's no way to talk to your King," Alastor seethes.

I go still, trying to compose myself and ignore the throbbing in my side.

He swings the rod and hits my other side. Pain shoots through my body as more ribs crack. I hold in a groan, imagine my teeth sinking into his neck and killing him.

"Bow," he orders. "Welcome to your new kingdom, Meg. Get used to it."

"Never," I say. My heart is beating hard against my broken ribs, my sides ache. The chains around my wrist are feeling incredibly heavy.

He taps the top of my head twice with the iron rod. I know better than to fuck with a head injury and no fresh blood in my future. I hate him, I hate this, but I must keep my brain in its rightful place.

I tip my head.

"As you should." Alastor turns and leaves the cell, the heavy door slamming shut behind him.

My mind races with thoughts of escape and vengeance. I close my eyes. This is not the end. The battle for my throne has just begun.

# Twenty

Alastor fell to the ground outside Meg's cell. The voice of Lucifer roared in his mind.

*Find my bones. Find my bones. Find my bones!*

He'd almost fallen apart in front of the throneless Queen. Sweat dripped down his back as he struggled to hold himself together. The voice of Lucifer was too much. It was driving him mad.

A breeze sifted through the dungeon, carrying whispers of anguish and misery. Alastor clenched his fists and pressed his knuckles to the stone floor, hoping the pain of bone on stone would help him drown out the demanding voice echoing in his mind.

*Find my bones...*

The voice softened to a whisper, still relentless, a constant presence that gnawed at his sanity. Alastor pressed his palms against his temples as if he could push the voice away. Lucifer's demands grew louder, more insistent.

*Find my bones. Find my bones. Find my bones.*

Alastor's breaths came in ragged gasps. He felt like a

puppet, pulled by strings he could not sever. Lucifer's demand felt like a crushing burden.

Alastor moved to his feet, stumbling forward, boots scraping on uneven stone floor. Each step felt like an eternity. Alastor's mind raced with memories of before. He'd finally gotten the skin trades back on track, he was making millions, selling souls, and securing a future at the table with higher Demons.

He'd finally dragged himself out of the downfall from dealing with Shay and her half-breed boyfriend. He never considered the throne of Hell, it was never on his list of goals. But Lucifer's demands changed everything. Now the Raven King was breathing down his neck because he wasn't making the soul quota and the Higher Demons of Hell had been promised skin, neither of which Alastor could focus on while dealing with this mess.

Alastor's jaw tightened as he mentally checked off the places he'd searched. He'd interrogated Demons, followed every whisper and rumor, and it all led him here to the castle in the burning caves. The bones remained elusive, a tantalizing prize just out of reach. Frustration burned within him, threatening to consume him. He made his way out of the dungeon and climbed the winding stairs. He passed the rotting body of Meg's Basilisk, bones and flesh from the war he'd brought here. He walked down the hall, passed the Hellion lair, and shoved open the doors to the courtyard. He sprinted a few quick steps before jumping into the dead tree in the center of the courtyard. He gripped branches above his head and pulled himself up. Alastor climbed until he could see over the canopy of the nearby forests. The depths of Hell seemed endless, a labyrinth of torment and darkness. Just the way he liked it. Somewhere in that infernal maze lay the remains of Lucifer, and with them, the power to be free.

*You are nothing without me,* Lucifer's voice said. *Remember that. Your strength, your purpose all stem from my will. Find my bones and you will be rewarded.*

With a roar of frustration, Alastor leapt from the tree branch. The winds howled around him but he welcomed the chaos, it matched the turmoil within his soul. He fell like a cat, landing on two feet with a heavy thump. The only reward Alastor wanted was freedom from the voice in his head. He began searching the grounds himself. He would find the bones, restore Lucifer and then... he would wrest his destiny from the clutches of his sperm donor.

While he searched, he contacted the Hellion families and called upon the next batch of Hellions bred to serve the throne.

# Twenty-One

*Meg*

THERE IS NOT much sense of time in this cell, but from the cramping in my stomach, I know it's been a few days. The cold stone walls press in on me, their dampness seeping into my bones. A single torch flickers in the hallway outside, casting erratic shadows through the small, barred window on the door.

Footsteps echo in the corridor, a constant reminder of my captivity. I've heard the changing of the guards, new Hellions taking their place, their guttural voices muttering as they pass by. It didn't take Alastor long to replace the ones he killed.

One Hellion sits outside my door now. I can hear his breathing; a harsh rasp that grates on my nerves. I wonder if he's bored or if he's waiting for something interesting to happen. But then, nothing about this place encourages curiosity or hope.

My stomach growls loudly, a painful reminder of my situation. I wonder if they'll ever feed me in this prison. Alastor has many ways to break a person, and starvation is one of the simplest–the easiest with me. It's a slow torment, gnawing away at strength and resolve. He knows I'm starving. Food has always been a hot point for me. Raised on starvation, it became worse when the need to consume blood overtook me all those years ago.

I shift slightly, the chains binding my wrists clinking softly. My thoughts wander, trying to focus on anything other than the hunger. I wonder if anyone will be looking for me. The chances of them finding me here, in this forsaken dungeon, feel terribly slim.

My throat is parched, each swallow a reminder of the thirst burning within me. I need a warm body, heck I'd suck on a blood popsicle right now, that's how low my standards are. I glance to the dried blood on the stone floor... No. Not that low. But... maybe.

My thoughts keep drifting to Skeele and his torn body on the floor of the Hellion lair. I've never let regrets run my life, but it's grim to not think about all the things I could have done differently when Alastor breached the castle walls.

The Hellion outside shifts, his armor clinking. I open my eyes, staring at the door. If he comes in, maybe I can overpower him, take his weapon. But even in my thoughts, the idea feels desperate and foolish. I'm too weak, my strength sapped by days of hunger and thirst.

My fingers trace the rough stone beneath me, feeling each crack and crevice. This cell, this tomb, feels like it's swallowing me whole. I can't let Alastor win. I have to hold on, have to believe that there's a way out of this nightmare. I've spent too much of my life locked up. Bitches always seem to want to lock me up. It started with John Lewis, then the Sheriff in Gouverneur, then those fucking Deacons, then Remiel, the Archangels... Damn the list goes on and on and makes me wonder why in the hell I didn't lock more people up in my dungeon. I put a pin in that shit for when I get out of here. Everyone who's ever looked at me sideways is going in a cell. I'll cage them and starve them and see how they like it.

The footsteps in the hallway continue, a grim symphony of my imprisonment. Each step is a reminder of my helplessness, each pause a punctuation to my despair. But the horrors persist and so do I. I must. For my children, for the memory of Skeele, for the chance to make Alastor pay for what he's done.

As the torchlight flickers and the hours drag on, I cling to that thought. I will survive this. Somehow. I'll find a rat or a... spoon. I've done that before, spooned my way out of lockup. I move my arms and tap the metal chains to a tune. After a few jangles I settle on Michael Jackson's *Beat It*.

I lean my head back against the wall, closing my eyes briefly. I won't be getting food while I'm here. Maybe I can get that Hellion to come closer to me and I can bite him. Yeah, that's my next plan. Bite the monster. Become the monster. Fuck shit up.

# Twenty-Two

Sparrow always knew where Alastor was, it was part of the deal with the Crossroads Demon or Demons, Shay and Nero. If Alastor were a needle in a haystack, Sparrow would find him. No matter what plane he was on Alastor was tracked, Earthen or Hell or Seven Kingdoms of Heaven–not that any Demon would be caught dead in Heaven.

Sparrow had been inside the castle in the burning caves before, knew it quite well after being Lucifer's Hellion for all that time he was trying to free his family from the curse of his father, the Archangel Remiel. It was a burden left for Sparrow. Remiel never did his required time as a Hellion, and as a result, his children were a bit crazy. Sparrow did his time–against Meg's wishes–in an effort to cure himself, Nightingale, and any future children of the curse.

A Hellion met Sparrow in the hall. The fucker was disgusting, definitely Hellions of a different time. Menacing, feral, trouble. These were the kind that killed first and asked questions later. These were the Hellions of Lucifer's reign returned. Sparrow wondered what happened here. Judging from the rotting flesh in the hall, and the destruction and smell, Alastor had taken the castle by force.

"Alastor, now," Sparrow told the Hellion.

The creature grunted and began walking. They passed the Hellion lair, the stairwell, the kitchen. The Hellion brought Sparrow to the ballroom, opened the door and grunted with the motioning of his hand. Sparrow entered.

The ballroom had been transformed into a disaster. There was broken furniture, holes in the walls, papers littering the floor, food rotted on tables. Haphazard blankets had been hung over the floor to ceiling windows letting in streaks of ochre light.

The sound of water sloshing echoed in the giant room. Sparrow followed the noise, footsteps making hollow noise as he rounded a mountain of broken chairs piled ten feet high. Alastor was kneeling at an out of place tub, his head underneath the water.

Sparrow walked closer, waiting to see if the Demon was possessed or looking to die. He glanced at the time, at the slow bubbles rising from the tub. Either Alastor had more self-control that he'd ever seen or something else was holding him under. Sparrow would give him a few more seconds before intervening. He didn't want the Demon dead–Sparrow had too much to collect from him. They had a deal for a transaction of souls to rebuild Sparrow's kingdom and power. Sparrow was nearly there; his seat in Babylon had grown by leaps and bounds, he had a say in plenty of decisions these days. He had more power than his father ever dreamed of having. No, Sparrow couldn't risk the death of Alastor, he'd have to pull the

Demon out of the water soon if the guy didn't do it himself.

Water flew through the air as Alastor whipped himself upright, his neck arching back, dark hair flying and spraying more water as he took a giant gulping breath. Water speckled the room and Sparrow's clothing.

"Are you stupid?" Sparrow asked.

Alastor laughed, water streaming from his hair, soaking his shirt. His chest expanded as he breathed deep, wiping off his face, then stood.

"More than stupid," Alastor finally said. He wasn't going to tell the Sparrow that the only way to stop Lucifer's voice was a near death experience. "What do you want?"

Sparrow wandered the once grand ballroom, taking in the desecration.

"I already sent the souls," Alastor said.

"You were short. A hundred less than last month." Sparrow scraped his heels as he walked, enjoying the sound against the elaborate tile flooring. "We have a deal."

"I have been preoccupied with this," Alastor said as he walked to a table with a map laid out.

"Questing?" Sparrow asked.

Alastor slammed his fists down on the table. "Lucifer wants his bones." He glanced at Sparrow, dark eyes desperate. "Do you know where they are?"

Sparrow clicked his tongue. "Afraid not." He smirked. Poor shit, Sparrow wasn't going to get involved in that horror show. "The souls."

"I'll get the numbers up again. Just as soon as I'm done here." Alastor moved to another table littered with glasses and liquor. He poured a half glass of bourbon like one would pour a glass of orange juice. He took a long swig before turning to Sparrow again. "I worked too hard to watch everything crash and burn again."

"We have a deal," Sparrow reminded Alastor.

"I know." Alastor paced, glass in hand. "You think I like being here? I don't. I want out. I want to be gone but I need those damn bones. No one has them. No one knows where they are." He pressed the glass to his forehead.

"I'm sure someone does," Sparrow said, biting his cheek. "Have you tried the Deacons?"

"They're all dead."

"Well that was a stupid decision." Sparrow tapped the map, rounded the table, and noted the markings. There were X's and scratches all over the parchment. It looked like Safe Houses and Hellion camps had been searched and checked off the list.

"Heard a rumor you caught Meg," Sparrow said, keeping his eyes on the map.

Alastor chuckled wickedly. "Wasn't that hard." He downed the rest of the bourbon. "Killing everyone around her was easy. She barely put up a fight."

"You killed everyone?" Sparrow's brow rose in interest. "Even her child?"

"There were no children in the castle. Searched every corner. Empty. Not even Shay nor that half-breed abomination."

"Haven't seen those two in a very long time," Sparrow muttered as he feigned interest in the map in an effort to distract him from the possibility of Meg's child being dead along with everyone else. The kid couldn't have been very old, barely a teenager by now. What a waste.

"But Meg's alive?" Sparrow asked.

"You could say that." Alastor headed toward the tub of water again.

"Babylon will be very interested in her."

"She's mine to deal with. I can't get rid of her until she tells me where Lucifer's bones are."

"She was unconscious when they were collected," Sparrow said.

"She knows where they are." Alastor knelt at the tub, ready to worship the silence. "He told me she knows."

Sparrow kept his tone even, relaying nothing in his words. "She is a trophy, one that Babylon would pay highly for."

Alastor took a deep breath, steadied himself on the edge of the tub and said, "Give me a minute."

Sparrow's brow and cheek ticked in curiosity. Once Alastor went under, shadows drifted from under Sparrow's black wings and around his feet. He paced the room, knowing he probably had a just a minute or two before Alastor came up for air and more conversation.

The sound of water splashing echoed. Sparrow mentally calculated Meg's worth in Babylon, nudging a pile of papers on the floor and controlling the tick that threatened to escape.

Alastor was drying his face with a towel this time as he walked toward Sparrow. "You want to see her?" he asked. "Meg in chains is a spectacle."

"Isn't she your niece?"

Alastor shrugged. "It's just a fact. Didn't say I wanted to screw her."

Something like rage flooded Sparrow's body at the

thought of Alastor touching Meg. He had half an urge to wrap his hands around Alastor's neck and force him to retract the statement. Sparrow shivered. He couldn't lose his cool. Not now. Not after everything.

Alastor threw the towel across the room and it landed haphazardly on a chair. "Lucifer says hello."

Sparrow nodded. "Show me Meg."

He wanted to make sure she was alive and would remain alive. She'd be worth a lot to Babylon. Sparrow calculated the souls she'd be worth, the power he could get for brokering her delivery to Babylon.

Sparrow followed Alastor as he itched his scalp and muttered to himself. The poor fuck was losing his mind. Maybe Sparrow should help him find the bones and put the Demon out of his misery so he could get back to the skin trades and delivering souls to Sparrow's kingdom.

# Twenty-Three

*Meg*

THERE ARE footsteps outside my cell. I don't have the energy to roll over and see who it is. The lack of blood has made me weak. Too weak. What I wouldn't do for a slice of pizza right now or a bag of blood. The dried blood on the floor is starting to look more appetizing by the minute. I glance at the dried blood and consider licking it off the floor.

The hinges of the door scream as it opens. Footsteps, a studder step. It's Alastor. I've recognized he can't walk more than a few steps these days without scraping his left foot across the floor. Something is wrong with him. He reminds me of a dog with fleas, always scratching his head and talking to himself. It seems the new King of Hell might have mange.

A small knife falls to the floor, landing in front of my face.

"Cut it off," Alastor says.

"My nose?" I ask, holding in a laugh, feeling as crazy as he is. Delusional even. I blame the lack of nutrition.

"The birthmark."

I roll to my back. "Not a tattoo or a scar or a limb. A birthmark." I look up at him and move my hands so the chains scrape across the stone floor.

Alastor's pointing to my upper thigh. "The birthmark. Cut it off," he demands. "I have a task for you and can't risk you disappearing on me."

My stomach clenches. I can't travel at will without fresh blood, I never considered the lack of the birthmark. It's small, looks like a snake eating its own head. The ouroboros gave me the power to flash between realms, but so did my father's blood. I am still Gabriel's daughter. Still the granddaughter of Lucifer. I take a deep breath, losing the birthmark might be nothing. Or, it could be *everything*.

Alastor kicks the knife closer to me. "Do it now. Stop wasting time." He paces a few steps. "Do it or I'll have one of my Hellions do it."

There's a growl from outside my cell. Something sinks in my gut. It sounds like the Hellions of old, the Hellions of Lucifer's rule. Those Hellions broke me, nearly killed me. Panic starts to rise in my chest, my throat feels full, and it's hard to swallow.

"Do it!" Alastor shouts.

"Fine." I sit up and grab the knife. What have I got to lose? My back aches from my broken wing. Only one side will fold in and lay flat, the other is twisted, the bone too far broke to reconnect and heal. If I had some blood it might heal itself. I grip the knife. Even if I make it out of here, I wouldn't get far with a broken wing and no blood, no ability to *poof* and travel at will. I'll be nothing but a mortal traipsing through Hell. I've been there once before.

"You gonna watch me take off my pants, you sick fuck?" I ask.

Alastor kicks me in the back, sharp pain erupts up my spine. "Do it. Or I'll stomp your good wing."

I shimmy out of my jeans, press the tip of the knife to the soft skin of my inner thigh, blood leaking. This is going to hurt like a bitch. But, I'll have a knife. It seems like a decent tradeoff considering my current situation.

I hiss at the pain of slicing my own skin. *This is nothing*, I tell myself, *you've lived through worse.* The birthmark is no bigger than a quarter but the hole in my thigh bleeds all over the floor.

"Give it," Alastor says.

I throw the skin at him and it lands on the floor by his shoes. He mutters something guttural as he bends down. Hellspeak. His fingertips ignite, burning the scrap of flesh in a minute.

"What was the significance of that?" I ask.

"Some thought it made you special. The ouroboros mark brings power. Now you're nothing special, no different than the rest of us monsters." Alastor looks down his nose at me. "Tragic, I could have made a killing off you in the skin trades, even with all those tattoos and scars. The higher Demons go feral for the trashy ones."

I'm paralyzed as he mouths off about how much he could sell me for, how many times, and to who. I try to remember their names so I know who to lock up first when I get on the other side of this ordeal.

Alastor waltzes out of the room. "Had you told me where his bones were..."

He never finishes, simply slams the door closed.

I tear a strip of fabric off my shirt and wrap it around the bleeding wound on my leg.

"Throw the knife toward the door," the Hellion says. "Stop the bleeding." The Hellion's tone changes and I know why. Fresh blood is difficult to ignore.

I was hoping they'd forget. I throw the knife overhand like a baseball and it lodges in the door, far from my reach. It stays there. No one opens the door to retrieve it.

I lay back on the stone floor and distract myself with memories of my children and consider where it all went wrong. Probably the moment I met Sparrow and trusted him with my life. Probably the second I fell in love with him.

# Twenty-Four

ALASTOR SAT ON THE OLD LEATHER CLUB CHAIR, his fingers drumming rhythmically on the armrest. The disheveled ballroom was eerily silent, save for the occasional crackle of fire and the distant wails of the damned drifting up from the dungeon. The air was thick with the stench of brimstone, and shadows danced on the walls, cast by the flickering torches.

The grand doors creaked open and Sparrow strode in, his eyes scanning the room before settling on Alastor. He was relieved that the Demon wasn't kneeling before the porcelain tub attempting to drown by baptismal bath again. A smirk tugged at the corner of Sparrow's lips as he approached the throne, his steps echoing through the cavernous space.

"Each time I come here I am impressed by the disarray," Sparrow said, his voice laced with mock admiration. "Suits you well."

Alastor's lips curled into a thin smile. "It's good to see

you. Finally someone who understands Lucifer's incessant nagging."

Sparrow chuckled, his eyes glinting with mischief. "Just thought I'd drop by and see how the new King of Hell is settling in. And of course, I'm curious about your progress with Lucifer's bones."

Alastor's expression darkened slightly, but he maintained his composure. "The bones are... elusive. But I'm making progress. Every day I get closer to finding them."

Sparrow raised an eyebrow, his smirk widening. "Elusive, you say? I suppose it's not easy tracking down pieces of the devil himself. Any leads?"

Alastor's fingers stopped drumming, and he leaned forward slightly. "I will find them. It's only a matter of time."

Sparrow nodded thoughtfully, his gaze never leaving Alastor's. "And when you do, you'll have your freedom."

"Babylon wants her," Sparrow said, watching Alastor closely. The Demon looked like shit and that was unlike him. Alastor was always dressed well, groomed, and styled like a Wall Street businessman. Now his suit was tattered, dress shirt untucked and buttoned wrong.

"No," Alastor said. "They can't have her, not until she tells me where Lucifer's bones are."

"After all this time," Sparrow took a deep breath, "if she hasn't told you after everything you've done to her, she doesn't know."

"You pity her," Alastor said.

"Not her." Sparrow crossed his arms over his chest, annoyed. "You owe me souls. Another month has passed and the soul count dwindles." Sparrow tipped his chin down. "Meg is a valuable asset. Her soul could pay off quite a few debts, don't you think?"

Alastor's gaze hardened, and he leaned back in the leather chair. "Don't play games with me, Raven King. I know the value of her soul. But she's more than just a bargaining chip. She's a thorn in my side and I will deal with her accordingly."

Sparrow raised his hands in mock surrender. "Of course, of course. I wouldn't dream of questioning your methods."

Alastor's hands tore through his hair. "Lucifer won't release me until I find his bones and bring him back."

"We have a deal," Sparrow reminded him. It was more than a deal and Sparrow had yet to show Alastor the hold he had over the Demon thanks to Shay and Nero. He was saving that for when it was really needed, for a dire situation, for when Alastor was so far out of place he needed a full reset. "Maybe get her out of the dungeon, that might help," Sparrow suggested. "You need more portals, stop bottlenecking the influx." Sparrow strode to the map that Alastor had been studying. He pointed to the one portal that remained about thirty miles to the west. "If you built even two more, it would be like Lucifer's days. Free trade, free movement. With the Deacons gone, the Earthen plane is yours to pillage. More souls for all of us. You need to catch up."

Alastor shook his head to stop the voice and moved to the table. He should set up Hell to function smoother once Lucifer took over again.

Sparrow noted new Xs on the map. There were only

two more Safe Houses that hadn't been checked for the bones.

Alastor was nodding in agreement to Sparrow's recommendation. The Demon didn't heed advice but his mental state was subpar these days. He'd probably jump out the window if Sparrow told him to.

"More portals are good. Meg destroyed most of them during the Fast-Zombie War." Alastor was nodding as he spoke, he rubbed his palms together. "I think I have an even better idea."

"If you need any assistance, I'm always here." Sparrow stepped back, ready to leave.

Alastor chuckled. "You're only slumming it down here because you want your souls and that's it. Why don't you help me find the bones?" Alastor slammed his fist on the table.

"I don't know a thing about his bones. I wasn't here for that." Sparrow backed away.

Alastor watched him go, a mixture of suspicion and determination in his eyes. The ballroom fell silent once more, the weight of their conversation lingering in the air like a dark, unspoken menace.

# Twenty-Five

*Meg*

The strip of fabric wrapped around my thigh has finally dried. I'm afraid to remove it. Afraid what little blood I have left will leak out and the Hellion outside my door will come inside looking for a meal.

I pick up my jeans and shake them. A few spiders scurry away. A shiver rolls up my spine. I could eat the spiders. I've eaten rats to survive. The thought leaves me as the dungeon door opens.

"Get dressed," Alastor orders. He crosses the room and releases my chains from the wall.

I stand and put my filthy jeans on, easing them over the wound on my thigh.

"Follow me," Alastor says, holding the chain like a leash.

"Where are you taking me?" I ask, stepping across the

threshold of the cell for the first time in weeks. I get a glance at the Hellion standing guard and immediately wish I'd never looked. He's pug-faced and warty with a headful of horns and sharp teeth curling out from his bottom lip.

I am led up the stairs and toward the door to the courtyard. The pug-faced Hellion follows closely and his presence makes me feel like I'm being chased by a boar.

Alastor opens the door to the courtyard. I see Hellsky for the first time in weeks. I raise a hand to shade my eyes against the ochre sun. It's not even that bright but my vision is acclimated to weeks of darkness.

I am taken to a Jeep and told to sit in the back, the chains around my wrists secured to a bolt in the floor. Alastor gets behind the wheel and pulls away from the castle. I turn, noticing another Jeep following. He drives down crumbling roads and past hordes of the dead, more than I've ever seen in this realm. I think of all the dead Deacons Alastor brought when he overtook the castle. I'm not one for worrying but these people don't deserve to be lost to Hell, they deserve their time to repent, for their souls to find peace in death. I scan the road and the forests, every turn, and every crumbling building. I wonder if Babylon has figured out what's going on here. What's taken them so long to investigate?

Alastor drives to a familiar place, a field where there used to be a portal. I destroyed it years ago with Skeele to prevent more of the Fast-Zombies from entering Hell.

Alastor stops the Jeep and gets out. He rounds the vehicle and opens my door, tugging me out by the chains.

"I have a little chore for you," Alastor says. He motions

to the piles of blasted stone. "Fix it. Once you're done with this, there's more. All of the ones you destroyed. Maybe the physical labor and fresh air will help you remember where your grandfather's bones are buried."

"You want me to rebuild a portal, alone, with no food or drink?" I ask.

"No, you won't be alone." Alastor motions to the Jeep behind us.

A Hellion exits the driver side, walks to the back of the vehicle, and opens the door. Someone gets out and there's a sinking in my gut. I'm worried that it's someone close; one of the children or Shay. Alastor has always had a thing for Shay. Or Jed. He's always had a hard on to kill Jed. The door slams.

Breath catches in my throat as the figure rounds the Jeep. It's Chel. His wings are tattered, he's thin–too thin– and haggard. There are cuts to his face and chest, scars etched into his arms and legs.

The plummeting realization hits me that he never made it to the last portal when the siege on the castle began, he never found help.

Chel is chained around his wrists just the same as I am and now I wonder if those cries of torment I heard in the dungeon were his. He is the last of my Hellions. The last of anyone who might be on my side in this realm. I try my best to tamp down the small flutter of hope.

Alastor unlocks one of my shackles and one of Chel's, then connects the chains together.

"There ya go. Help." Alastor turns to look at me. "Big strong Hellion to help you lift the heavy rocks." He points to the road. "When you're done here, there's more to piece together."

There's shuffling in the forest.

"You're going to leave us out here with no weapons and the dead wandering? I am no longer the Queen of Hell, they'll come for us," I remind him.

Alastor shrugs. "You'll figure it out."

Alastor and his Hellion retreat to the Jeeps and drive away. I barely believe it. Fresh air, sunlight, near freedom.

Chel comes at me. His face is hard to read. I backstep. A sad smile escapes his lips as he folds both arms around me.

"I'm sorry," Chel says.

"Don't be sorry," I say. "We tried." I always hated being touched but nothing has ever felt more wonderful than Chel's arms squeezing me.

"I failed." Chel releases me, setting me on my feet.

I look away, ashamed. "I failed bigger. The biggest."

Chel sniffs the air before his eyes zero in on the blood soaking through my jeans. "You're injured. Did they..." his face drops. "What did they do to you?"

I force an uncomfortable laugh. "I'm fine. It's just... a wound. He made me cut off the birthmark."

Chel makes a face, not understanding.

"It helped me *poof*," I say. "I'm not sure if I'll ever be able to travel like that again."

Chel shrugs. "You're alive at least. That's all that matters."

"I'm not so sure." There's shuffling in the nearby forest. "Maybe we should be quiet until nightfall. Work when the dead are asleep."

"That would draw less attention." Chel scans the grassy

area and the tree line. "I'd rather run away. Get to safety." He moves his arm and the chain clangs. "The other portal is not far."

I shake my head. "We are no longer safe in Hell. Did you see Alastor's Hellions?" I swallow hard, remembering. "Those are the worst kind."

"I know," Chel says. "My father was one."

A moment passes between us. He glances at my left wing. "What happened there?"

"Too broken to heal." I look away, trying to ignore the throbbing in my leg and my back, my head and my heart.

"Want me to do something for it? Do you want my blood?" He holds out his arm.

I glance back at him, lifting my arm so the chain connecting us clatters. "Nah, we got bigger fish to fry." I move closer to the giant pieces of cement and rock that were once a portal to cross into other realms. "How long do you think it will take us to do this?"

"A few days." He glances at me. "How weak are you?"

"I'm fine," I lie. The thought of drinking from him, of risking the bloodlust, of risking a blood bond, makes me want to vomit. I can't do that again. It's too dangerous. I'd rather die or be eaten by the dead than go down that road again.

We sit in the tall grass and wait for nightfall. Nearby a horde of the dead all fall with a *thump*, asleep at last.

"Let's get to work," I say, moving to stand. My left wing falls, grinding bone against soil, stretching the thickly scarred skin. I hiss in pain.

"You gotta fix that," Chel warns.

"Someday. If Alastor doesn't kill me first."

I start moving rocks, arranging them in the arch and matching up the runes like a giant puzzle.

"Alastor won't kill you, Meg," Chel says. "You're worth too much to all the realms." He groans, lifting a large chunk of the portal and moving it into place.

"I think you're wrong." I'm glad for the darkness so he can't see my expressions.

# Twenty-Six

Sparrow treaded cautiously through the shadowed corridors of Babylon, his footsteps echoing softly against the stone walls that delineated his realm from Gabriel's. Once, he and Teari had been allies, bound by friendship and a shared purpose. But that was before Sparrow's betrayal, before he'd chosen a darker path that led him away from those he once called friends.

Teari approached, walking instead of flying. Sparrow's heart raced with uncertainty. He knew he was treading on dangerous ground, seeking aid from someone he'd wronged so grievously.

Sparrow announced his presence with a heavy foot fall, his voice barely more than a whisper. Teari startled, her expression a mask of cool indifference.

"Raven King," Teari greeted, her voice tinged with a hint of disdain. "To what do I owe the pleasure of your visit?"

"I need your help."

Teari's eyebrow arched in skepticism. "My help?" she

repeated, her tone laced with sarcasm. "I went to you for help and you slammed the door in my face."

Sparrow stepped back, remembering the day Teari sought him out. The Raven King had plenty of dark days in which he struggled to step into the light. Unfortunately, she had approached him on one of those days.

"I have a question," Sparrow said.

"Okay." Teari's gaze softened slightly, though suspicion still lingered in her eyes. "I have places to be," she warned. "Hurry up."

Sparrow met Teari's gaze. "What is the treatment for drinking blood from the walking dead?"

"Who would do that?" Teari asked, unbelieving he'd have the audacity to ask her such a thing.

"Consider it a hypothetical."

"Did you do that?" Teari's eyes went wide as she inspected him closely. "Did you?"

"Not me."

Teari didn't like where this conversation was going. If it wasn't Sparrow then it was someone he knew or wanted to poison.

"Do you know the cure?" Sparrow asked again.

"You could ask your kingdom's healer," Teari said.

Sparrow exhaled an annoyed breath. "I don't have one."

"Sounds like a problem," she scoffed. Teari glanced over her shoulder, hoping no one caught her speaking with Sparrow. She didn't want Gabriel to know and lose his trust in her. She'd worked too hard for Gabriel to do that. "Look, I'm busy. I have to go."

A hand reached out to stop her. "What do you want for the information?" Sparrow finally asked.

"Where is Meg?" Teari asked.

Sparrow's lips pressed together in a tight line. "Who is that?"

"You should do better," Teari warned.

Sparrow rushed towards her, his face an inch from her nose, shadows and anger swelled around his body. "You know nothing," he seethed. "Not a single thing. Don't stand there with your white wings and pride and think you are so much better than me." His hands had curled into fists and he shifted his big body, wanting to strangle her where he stood.

"No, Sparrow," Teari replied flatly. "It's you who know nothing." She turned on her heel and stepped across the boundary to Gabriel's kingdom. Guilt flooded her when she realized someone might actually be suffering. "Tincture of time is your answer," she shouted over her shoulder. "There is no other cure."

# TWENTY-SEVEN

NIGHTINGALE, NOAH, AND THRUSH EXITED THE fountain in the center of Babylon. Noah turned, taking in his surroundings.

"Do ethereal creatures belong here?" Noah asked.

"I don't care," Nightingale replied. "Follow me." She skated over the water, turning to a stop before stepping down from the fountain.

"Why you always gotta skate all fancy-like?" Noah asked Nightingale, appreciating the short shorts. "Why can't you just walk like the rest of us schmucks?"

"Because it's boring," Nightingale replied with an unimpressed tone.

Thrush stepped over the ledge of the fountain, his soaked clothing leaving puddles as he walked. His parents were dry, like they'd never been submerged. Thrush followed the two toward a stone walkway. The lingering Angels of Babylon began noticing them and moving closer.

What Thrush couldn't see was the steam rising off his body like smoke, he didn't notice the smell of woodsmoke and pine. He didn't smell like Heaven, he smelled like Hell and everyone within a certain radius noticed. He didn't belong there and it was blatantly obvious.

Thrush took in every motion of the surrounding crowd that had gathered to watch them. Thrush hadn't been to the Seven Kingdoms of Heaven since he was an infant. He wasn't sure what to expect, but he'd been trained by the strongest Hellions in Meg's court so he didn't miss one hand movement, one step fall, or one motion in his periphery. He gripped the small blade at his hip and adjusted the bag on his shoulder. He wondered if they'd try and attack. Sure that he could take out a handful of them by himself, he worried if anyone would come to their rescue if an Angel attack overwhelmed him. He glanced at his parents. They'd have to draw on their Astral magic to protect him. Thrush hid his limp, not favoring his sore ankle that had twisted during their escape. He didn't want the Angels to notice any weakness.

"How far?" Noah asked.

"Maybe twenty minutes," Nightingale slowed to walk next to Thrush, his clothes drying quickly under the heat of Heaven's skies. The sun was intense.

They stopped at the gates leading to the Raven King's lands.

"Brother," Nightingale called. "Let us in, please."

Sparrow appeared in the distance, walking down a long winding driveway, toward the gate. Nightingale was shocked at the sight of her brother. It had been years since she'd last seen him. He'd given them peace in Meg's realm, promised ceasefire. The smirk on his face led Nightingale to believe that everything was about to change.

Sparrow stood at the gate, his hand resting on the lock. "Shouldn't you both be in the Ethereal realm?" he looked from Nightingale to Noah before his eyes landed on Thrush.

"Let us in," Nightingale said.

"Just send the boy," Sparrow's eyes narrowed on Thrush. "He's due for training. He needs to be prepared for his future now that you've changed sides. He's been away from his rightful home for too long."

Nightingale called upon the same ethereal power she used to defeat the Nightjar. She began to illuminate, drawing light from the sun until her body glowed brightly.

"Neat trick," Sparrow said as he unlocked the gate and pushed it open.

"Raven King," Nightingale said. "This land is as much his as it is yours. This is family land. We are refugees of war."

Sparrow stepped back and motioned for them to enter. "What happened to Hell?" Sparrow glanced at her scarred cheek.

"We've been banished," Nightingale said, her voice cold. She had an urge to remind her brother that the scars came from her death, bitten in the neck and face by the Fast-Dead.

Noah glared at Sparrow. "I remember a time when you weren't such a dick."

The corner of Sparrow's mouth tipped up in a half smile. Noah took that as a good sign. Maybe under Sparrow's dark façade he wasn't so different. Noah had seen the masks Meg had to wear as the Queen of Hell. There was a time that Sparrow and Noah were friends when Sparrow was doing his time as a Hellion and remained devoted to Meg. Times had changed. Still, it was hard for Noah to understand what Sparrow had turned into after all these years. He'd went from quirky and fun to dark and serious.

The lock to the gate clicked closed. Nightingale turned. "Thrush, this is your uncle Sparrow," Nightingale motioned to the Raven King.

Sparrow held out a hand toward Thrush. "Haven't seen you since you were a baby. You're practically grown now."

Thrush placed his hand in Sparrow's, wary with his free hand on the hilt of his hidden knife.

Sparrow glanced to the boy's hip and noted the weapon. One brow rose in interest. "Seems you've had some training."

Thrush smiled and it was just as dark as Sparrow's. Thrush wouldn't hesitate to draw a weapon, didn't want his uncle to think he had the upper hand, King or not.

"Don't mind Sparrow," Nightingale warned. "He went crazy a few times. But you can thank him for breaking the family curse." Nightingale touched the back of Thrush's head. "He's the reason why you aren't cracked in the head like the rest of us."

"Jury's still out on if it was a curse." Sparrow released Thrush's hand and began walking, black wings scraping the road in a constant *shhhhhh*.

Nightingale gave Sparrow a dirty look, and Noah stayed protectively close to Thrush.

A house appeared in the distance. These were not the family lands Nightingale remembered. Their home was gone, destroyed in the Fast-Zombie War. That was also where Nightingale died, bit in the neck by the dead. Then

Jack, Noah's brother, was bit. Meg rescued Thrush–kidnapped him really–and brought him to Hell.

Nightingale held back emotion. Returning to this place brought back too many memories and the realization of missed time after she'd died and strangers were left to raise her child. Nightingale moved closer to Thrush as they neared the house.

"I wasn't expecting guests," Sparrow said as he opened the door to the house. "Wait here while I have one of the surrounding cabins prepared."

Nightingale noted it wasn't as grand as their father's house. There were fewer levels, it reminded her of a large cabin. She wondered if the underground levels where their father had kept her locked up for most of her life remained. Nightingale decided she wouldn't ask right now, maybe later.

Noah got Nightingale's attention. "Do you think this is safe?" he mouthed.

"It's all we've got." She focused on Thrush. "We can't take our son to the Ether and the Earthen plane is too dangerous." Nightingale shuddered at the thought of going to Babylon and begging another Archangel to give them sanctuary. She might be dead but she had some pride still.

———

Sparrow led them to a small cabin not far from the main house. "Make yourselves at home," he said as he opened the door and entered. "Some things are similar to the way father ran the kingdom. The fridge will remain stocked. Clothes cleaned." He turned to look at Thrush. "You can start training with the Legion in the morning."

Thrush nodded. His ankle throbbed and he couldn't wait to put it up and rest.

"Are the training grounds in the same location?" Nightingale asked.

Sparrow nodded. "Welcome home, sister and family." He closed the door and left them alone.

Noah exhaled a large sigh. "Jesus Christ," his eyes were wide as he focused on Nightingale, "is it always this suffocating here? Everything is so quiet and proper and stoic and hot." He ran hands through shaggy blonde hair. "How did you survive this most of your life?"

Nightingale smirked. "Now you see why I was so eager to follow Meg to Hell. And don't worry, it will only get worse. You've only met one person so far."

"Yeah but there's a *vibe*." Noah rolled his eyes before nudging Thrush. "You doin' okay with all this?"

Thrush shrugged. "The Raven King sees me as a threat."

"No, no," Nightingale soothed. "He's just had his brains scrambled too many times." She rubbed Thrush's arms trying to calm him.

"Maybe we should have taken our chances with Alastor," Thrush suggested before saying, "I'm gonna find my room."

Thrush walked away from his parents to explore the cabin.

"He's just a teenage boy," Noah said to Nightingale. "We just took him away from the only home he's ever known. And the only friends he's ever had."

Nightingale never had any friends as a child so she couldn't relate much, but she nodded remembering the joy she felt when Meg visited that first time.

———

Thrush found a room in the back of the cabin. There was a large window that faced the forest and a private bathroom. He threw his bag on the floor before bending to unpack his things. He pulled out the books, wishing he'd wrapped them in something waterproof. The pages were soggy and limp. He set them out to dry and hoped they'd regain their original shape. He shook out his clothing and hung them to dry. Opening a small, zippered pocket, he took out a charcoal pencil and a pouch of salt and a small notebook with spells. The notebook hadn't fared so well after getting wet. He gripped the charcoal pencil and flipped through the pages, landing on a rune he knew quite well. He closed his eyes, remembering the door casings of their home in Hell. Then he began to etch the door and the window casings with charcoal. When he was done, he took out one of the small blades given to him by the Hellions and began carving runes into the wood of the cabin. Thrush wasn't about to risk his life to the Raven King's lands.

# TWENTY-EIGHT

*Meg*

WE FINISH the portal in two days. Just as Chel is fitting the keystone into place, the sound of tires crunching on concrete approaches.

Chel groans as he drops the stone into place. The runes illuminate for a moment and a transparent sheen wavers between the arch.

"Strong work," I try to joke with Chel, but it comes out sounding patronizing. "Sorry, I'm tired."

Chel nods, understanding. Neither of us have eaten. We found crabapples at the tree line but they were sour and hard to bite. Neither of us wanted the gut ache that would come from eating them.

We turn and watch the vehicles approach. They park nearby and Alastor and one of his Hellions walk toward us.

Alastor slow claps. "You did it in record time. Keep up this pace and we'll have all the portals up and functioning again." He reaches in his pocket and pulls out two vials. "A reward for your hard work."

I glance at Chel. Alastor is holding out two vials of blood. My mouth waters. I don't even care where the blood came from, I'm so hungry I'd drink blood from a worm, if worms had blood. I don't know if they do, but if they did, I'd drain them.

We each take a vial.

"Drink up," Alastor says. "You'll need your strength for the next portal."

We both pop the top off the vials, thirsty, hungry, parched beyond what we've ever been in a long time. It's not a lot of blood for either of us, just enough to wet our tongues and keep moving.

Chel drops his vial, his hand moving to his throat. He turns to look at me, panic in his eyes. "It's from the dead," he chokes out.

Dread hits me. I already drank mine, threw it back like a shot of whiskey. My stomach punches and bile rides up my throat. I bend over and vomit. Thin blood drips on the dirt. I rub my face and feel wetness as blood runs from my nose and eyes and ears. My head feels foggy and full. I drop to the ground, and easy on my left wing I force myself to fall face first into the grass. The ground vibrates as Chel drops, both of us gagging and choking and bleeding from our eyes.

Alastor laughs. "Are you ready to tell me where your grandfather's bones are now?"

I can't speak, can't make a noise. I can only gurgle and decide it's not worth trying to reply to him.

Alastor watches us writhe in pain. And when the worst

of it has passed, Alastor's Hellion drags us to the back of his Jeep and tosses us in.

———

We are dropped at the next broken portal site still barely functioning. My head feels like exploding, my throat is on fire, my stomach is churning. I didn't really believe it when I was told blood from the dead would make me sick.

"Get this done," Alastor motions to the rocks on the ground.

Not long after they leave, Chel is able to sit up, still gagging and retching. He takes deep breaths, apologizes when he lifts his arm and it jerks the chain attached to my wrist.

"It's okay," I mutter, moving to sit.

There are shuffling footsteps moving closer.

"They must like the sound of me puking." Chel stands, ready to fight.

I move to my feet, still feeling woozy. There's three of the dead headed our way. There's no way we can run.

"I got them," Chel says, "you stay behind me."

I reach for my blade, cursing when my hand comes in contact with my jean-clad thigh. My blade was lost after the battle in the Hellion lair.

A dead man wanders closer, mouth open and ready to bite. Chel steps forward and punches the man in his throat so hard his head snaps to the side and he drops to the ground.

He does this twice more and I think of how nice it would have been to have Chel around last time I was wandering Hell as nothing but a lost soul all those years ago. He makes killing the walking dead look easy.

"Look," I point to one of the corpses on the ground. The guy looks like he was a lumberjack or something with his flannel shirt and Carhart pants. "He has a hatchet."

Chel crouches down, grabs the hatchet and rips it free of the zombie. "This could come in handy."

"Yeah," I nod in agreement. "I'd like to chop off Alastor's head with it."

Chel chuckles. "Maybe." He turns to look at the ruins of the portal then glances at the chain linking us together. "Let's do this now, faster."

"What are you thinking?" I ask.

"Thinking like I'm already over this shit."

"Same."

We make fast work of the portal. Thankfully the chunks of rock are bigger. We finish by the time the moon is high in Hellsky. Then we stand side by side, watching the portal come to life.

Chel bends and picks up the hatchet from where he set it while we were working.

"What are you doing?" I ask.

"We can't stay chained together like this," Chel says, gripping the handle of the hatchet.

I lift my arm, jingling the chain. "Not possible. I don't have a key."

He crouches, laying his arm on the ground, his other hand gripping the hatchet. "In a moment it will be."

In a swift movement, Chel cuts off his hand.

"What the fuck!" I shout at him. "You could have warned me."

He stands, groaning, blood spurting. "You would have told me not to." He nods toward the portal. "You go first."

I hold up my arm and his lost hand falls from the shackle. "Do you want your hand?"

Chel picks it up and tucks it in his pocket as his arm bleeds profusely. He stumbles.

"You need to go first," I say. "You need to go to the Earthen plane. To the Peabody Library."

"What's there?" he asks.

"Friends." I lay a hand on his shoulder and push him toward the portal. "Go. I'll follow."

"You go next, Meg." He's watching me closely. "As soon as I'm gone, you better step through this portal."

I nod. "I will."

He glances at me one last time, a sickly pallor taking over his skin.

"Go," I urge.

"You did everything you could do," Chel says and then he steps through the portal.

I shiver, pushing away the thought that this was too easy. The sound of wings flapping fills the night sky. A Hellion hovers nearby. I catch a glimpse of its shadow.

I stand alone, moving away from the portal, the weight of the chain attached to my arm a constant reminder of the battles to come. The air is still, the eerie silence a prelude to the chaos that's about to hit me head on.

The sky darkens further, the Hellion's shadow eclipsing the ochre sun. I look up, squinting against the glare. The Hellion plummets from the sky, wings spread wide, moving with terrifying speed.

I brace myself, twisting my wrist to wrap the chain in

my palm. It clinks ominously as I wrap it tighter in my grip. The Hellion lands with a thunderous crash, the force of its impact sending a shockwave through the ground and nearly knocking me off my feet. Dust and debris swirl around us creating a momentary veil obscuring the Hellion's form.

Memories of Lucifer's Hellions rush me and a cold shiver of fear runs up my spine. I never stood a chance against those monsters, and definitely not now. This Hellion is massive, easily twice my height with skin like charred stone and eyes that burn with a hellish fire. It roars a sound that reverberates through my bones. It takes a step toward me, blade ready and claws extended, ready to rend flesh.

I don't give it a chance, I strike first with a swift motion I swing the chain in a wide arc, aiming for its kneecaps. The chain whistles through the air like a deadly serpent of iron and fury. It connects with the Hellion's knee, hitting that soft spot in the back of the leg, causing the Hellion's leg to give. It stumbles but quickly regains footing, snarling with rage.

"You're going to have to do better than that," I taunt, yanking the chain.

The Hellion lunges at me, claws and blade slashing through the air. I duck and roll to the side, narrowly avoiding its deadly strike.

I spring to my feet, using the momentum to swing the chain again, this time aiming higher. The chain wraps around the Hellion's arm. I pull with all my might but I'm not much of a match for the beast. It's muscles bulge and it snaps sharp teeth in my direction.

With a roar of defiance, the Hellion yanks its arm free,

the force of the motion sending me sprawling to the ground, knocking the wind out of me. I struggle to catch my breath and taste blood as my lip splits against the rough terrain.

The Hellion is on me in an instant, blade descending in a deadly arc. Guess Chel was wrong, they don't mind me being dead.

I roll to the side and the Hellion's blade hits dirt. I swing the chain again, aiming for its neck. It wraps around his throat and I pull with all my might, using the chain to leverage myself to my feet.

The Hellion chokes, eyes blazing with fury.

"You're strong," I say, tightening my grip on the chain. "But I once fought a dog for a peanut butter and jelly sandwich; this isn't much different. I've had practice."

The Hellion stops clawing at the chain around its neck and smiles at me before reaching for the chain.

My eyes go wide and a sickening feeling rushes my stomach as I see his wings spread wide. He bends his knees and launches himself into the sky, dragging me along.

I only have one functioning wing and this Hellion is fast. He wraps his wrist around the chain and swings me to the side. Soon it's like I'm on a carnival ride and ready to lose my lunch, except I never ate lunch and this is absolute bullshit.

The Hellion's wings flash up and he starts dropping. He's ready to smash me onto the ground. My stomach flip-flops. I spread one wing to lessen the blow. I try to stretch the other, groaning against the pull of broken bone, damaged tendons, and aching muscle. I'm not fast enough.

The Hellion yanks the chain and slams me onto my

back next to the portal. My vision blurs as I look up at Hell-sky. Blood drips from my lip and ears. I steel myself for whatever comes next as I hear the Hellion drop the chain to the ground with a heavy thud. Yes, Chel was very wrong. This Hellion is going to finish me.

There's a noise beside me, a whisper. My vision blurs and I see blobs of black. I think I have a concussion, maybe even brain damage because I see a hand reaching through the portal, wrap around my wrist, and pull me through just as everything turns to black.

# TWENTY-NINE

Shay stood in the grassy plains of Montana, the vast expanse of open sky stretching endlessly above her. The air was crisp, it smelled like wildflowers and pine and snow, a stark contrast to the scent of creosote and woodsmoke of Hell's atmosphere. Shay felt the familiar reins in her hands, and beneath her, the powerful, steady presence of Nero.

She urged Nero into a gentle trot, the rhythmic thudding of his hooves a soothing melody. The landscape rolled out before her, serene and untouched, a haven of peace that she longed to hold onto. In the distance, she recognized the family ranch, warm and inviting. So unlike the way she'd left it; saturated with blood and gore, zombies and her parents buried in shallow graves in the pasture. This was another memory. This was how her parents would want her to remember their home. The sun cast a golden glow over everything, making the world shimmer with warmth and light.

As they rode, Shay felt a deep sense of contentment

wash over her. This was home, always would be, a place where her worries seemed to dissolve into the gentle breeze. She leaned forward, running a hand along Nero's strong neck, feeling the smoothness of his coat and the strength of his muscles.

"Good boy," she whispered.

But as they rode further, the dream began to shift. The sky darkened, clouds gathered ominously. Shay felt a chill creep into the air. Nero's ears flicked back, sensing the change. Shay glanced around, trying to pinpoint the source of her unease, hoping that the dead nor Alastor's Demons were coming to infect her dream.

It was then Shay saw her–Nightingale–standing alone in the middle of the field, her presence both startling and familiar. The ethereal glow that surrounded her cast an eerie light, making her stand out against the darkening sky.

Nero disappeared and Shay was on her feet. Her boots crunched on the dry grass as she approached Nightingale.

"What are you doing here?" Shay asked. "This is my dream."

"You gave me permission a long time ago. And... I need your help. I'm searching for Meg." Nightingale's gaze locked onto Shay's and the dream world seemed to hold its breath.

"Meg?" Shay asked.

The dream began to collapse, the world around them faded into darkness. There was a pounding sound that echoed.

Shay woke, startled. Jed was already moving out of bed and pulling a shirt on.

"Someone is at the door," Jed warned. His fingertips flexed and sparks flew.

The pounding continued, more frantic now. Jed approached the door cautiously, sparks flying from his fingers, a battle spell on the tip of his tongue. He motioned for Shay to stay back, then bent and made a marking on the floor.

No one had come to the door of the abandoned Peabody Library since they'd lived here. The building was warded with protection spells, even more since they'd taken Meg's children into hiding.

"Who is it?" Jed asked, unsure if the person knocking could hear him through the hundred's years old wooden door.

"Chel," a gruff voice replied.

Shay's eyes went wide. "Open it," she said.

Jed pulled the heavy door open, and a shadowy figure, hunched and clutching something to his chest, lingered a moment before stepping inside.

"Holy shit," Chel said. "This is where you two have been hiding?"

Jed slammed the door closed, locking it and drawing new runes. It was the first time they'd opened the door and he hoped the last. Jed didn't want the humans of the Earthen plane noticing that the library wasn't really abandoned.

Chel stumbled and fell to his knees inside the rune circle on the floor, stuck. Blood dripped from his right wrist. His hand was missing and there was no bandage to stop the bleeding.

Shay gasped, rushing to Chel's side, "What happened?"

Chel's face was pale, pain and fear etched into every line. "Alastor chained us together. He made us rebuild the portals. It was the only way to free Meg." He glanced at the door. "She should have been right behind me."

Jed broke the rune circle on the floor, releasing Chel. The Hellion tipped over on his side and rolled to his back with a groan.

"Um," Shay picked up the giant hand that had fallen out of his pocket. "Is this your hand?" she asked with a gulp.

"Oh yeah," Chel chuckled faintly. "I used a hatchet to cut it off. You should've seen Meg's face."

"Alastor didn't do this to you?" Jed asked.

Chel made a noise of exasperation. "Hell no. I did it." He was staring at the door, expectantly. "She was supposed to be directly behind me. She made me go first." He closed his eyes.

"There's blood everywhere," Shay said.

"The castle is overrun. There's no one left," Chel said, blinking slowly.

Jed kneeled next to Chel, he took the severed hand and lined it up with Chel's wrist, then he chanted words that sounded like beach sand sifting between rocks and shells on a cold night. Tendrils of healing magic sprung from his fingertips and began mending Chel's severed limb. It staunched the bleeding and began knitting the blood vessels, muscle and bone back together.

Chel winced in pain.

"Sorry," Jed muttered between words.

Shay took Chel's free hand, her touch gentle but firm.

"You're safe here, for now," she assured him. "We'll figure out the next move together."

Jed looked at Shay, their eyes meeting in silent understanding. This wasn't just about Chel or Meg, the war in Hell was spilling over into the Earthen plane, and they couldn't ignore it any longer. They had precious cargo to keep safe. More creatures were on the Earthen plane than ever before now that word had spread about the double auras. And now there was a Hellion, battered and broken. Shay glanced at his tattered leathery wings. They shouldn't be visible on the Earthen plane, but Shay was looking right at them which meant the Veil was thinning considerably.

"Can you get the med kit?" Jed asked Shay.

She nodded and got up to retrieve it, her mind racing.

Chel closed his eyes, finally allowing himself a moment of respite. He took deep breaths, opening his eyes again when Shay settled next to him and passed Jed items from the med kit. Jed wrapped Chel's wrist and hand then splinted it. Chel gave him a questioning look.

"The magic is good, but I've never done that before." He folded Chel's arm against the Hellion's chest. "Just to be safe. You'll be sore."

Chel wiggled his fingers. "Seems to have worked."

Light footsteps shuffled from behind a bookshelf.

"Who's there?" Shay asked, squinting in the darkness.

The girl walked out; Rue with her dark hair mussed and pajamas wrinkled. "I heard voices."

Chel's eyes went wide and he struggled to sit up. "Are they both here?"

Jed pressed a hand on Chel's shoulder, preventing him from getting up. "Easy."

"You shouldn't be out here," Shay warned. "What if it was a Demon, one of the bad ones?"

Rue stared at Chel. "But I know him. He's not bad."

Tears glistened in the old Hellion's eyes as he reached toward Rue. "Your momma hid you well. Is your brother here also?"

Rue nodded. "He's asleep. He'll sleep through anything."

Jed made a face. "The only problem is, now you're stuck here too."

"No," Chel argued. "I have to get back out there and find Meg."

Jed shook his head. "No, you're not leaving until we have some more answers. Meg didn't want a soul to know about this place. Now you're here."

"She sent me here. She said I'd find friends." Chel rubbed his face with his good hand.

"Can't risk it," Jed said, magic crackling from his fingertips. "We don't have the resources to fight Hell's war here. We'll find another way to get Meg."

Chel nodded, understanding.

Jed placed a reassuring hand on Chel's shoulder. "Rest. Recover."

———

SHAY SAT in a quiet corner of the Peabody Library, the soft glow of the lamp illuminating the pages of the ancient tome spread out before her. Across the table, Jed was meticulously organizing a stack of scrolls by order of spells, his brow furrowed in concentration. Chel, meanwhile, paced back and forth near the window, his eyes scanning the darkening street outside.

"It's too quiet," Chel muttered, breaking the silence. "I don't like it."

Jed looked up, a flicker of concern crossing his face. "We can't afford to let our guard down," he agreed. "Especially not now." He glanced at the children sitting near the fire.

Shay sighed, closing her book with a thud. "I just feel like I'm waiting for the next disaster," she said, her voice tinged with frustration.

Chel paced closer to the table where Shay was reading, paused, and watched Rue and Remington near the fire, engrossed in their own studies.

"Shay," Chel began, his voice low but insistent. "What's with the tattoos on the kids?"

Shay looked up, her brow furrowing. "What about them?"

Chel lowered his voice. "They didn't have tattoos the last time I saw them in Hell. Those are powerful runes, not something to be used lightly, especially on children."

"We had no choice," Shay said. "They went outside and their auras drew the attention of every Demon nearby. It was like a beacon, alerting every dark creature to their presence on the Earthen plane."

Jed had moved closer, hearing the conversation. "The runes are the only way to protect them, to dampen their light enough to keep them hidden from those who seek to harm them."

Chel frowned, crossing his arms over his chest. "Do they know the significance of the runes? Do they understand why they were marked?"

"They understand," Jed replied. "They're okay."

Shay turned the page of her book. "Just because they're smaller than you does not mean they're babies. They understand. If they lived here they'd be away from their parents more than half the day at school and activities. Heck, you helped train them and took Remington on missions."

Chel's gaze softened slightly as he looked at the children, who were oblivious to the weight of the conversation happening around them. "You're right. They just look so small."

"They're not," Shay reminded him.

Chel exhaled a breath. "If the runes fail or the Demons find another way to track them, we'll need more than just tattoos to keep them safe."

Jed nodded, his expression grim. "For now the runes are our best defense. We'll do whatever it takes to protect them, even if it means facing down every Angel and Demon that crosses into this plane."

Chel's gaze lingered on the children for a moment longer before he turned back to Shay and Jed. "Let's hope it doesn't come to that. But if it does, you'll have my support. We'll protect them together."

Rue was suddenly standing next to Chel. He jumped, startled at her presence.

"Did you see my mother before you came?" Rue asked. "Is she alive?"

Chel kneeled so they were eye to eye. "I did see her." He held Rue's hands, remembering how small they once were, recognizing that she was indeed older and sturdier than the toddler he'd held upright while she learned to walk. "She is alive. We'll get her back," he promised.

Rue was staring into the Hellion's eyes, searching for truth like children do. "Is she hurt?"

"A tiny bit. Just a scratch." Chel shook his head. "She's strong. She'll be better soon."

"How do you know?" Rue frowned. "We should go find her together."

"Well, our friends here are going to keep you and your brother safe." Chel was running out of things to say. He was a Hellion after all, not gifted in the use of neutral language.

Rue released Chel's hands and walked away, muttering something about not being a baby anymore.

"Haven't felt that in a while," Shay said, glancing to Jed, her expression resolute.

Jed and Chel exchanged a worried glance.

Jed reached out and grasped her arm, his eyes filled with concern. "Be careful, Shay-baby," he urged, his voice a whisper to the children couldn't hear. "We don't know who or what we're dealing with."

Shay nodded, her heart pounding in her chest. "I will," she promised. With one last look at her friends Shay and Nero were pulled away and disappeared, the library's warmth replaced by the chill of the unknown.

———

SHAY AND NERO stood at the crossroads in a dark forest, the moon the only light. Shrouded by mist and shadow, the oppressive silence was broken only by the distant howl of a wolf in the mountains. As if on cue, a sudden chill spread over Shay and the faint smell of sulfur wafted through the air. Shay's eyes widened as a dark figure materialized outside the rune circle that had drawn them. A Demon appeared with eyes like burning coals and a sinister grin that sent shivers down her spine.

The Demon hissed, its voice like nails on a chalkboard.

"Who summons?" Shay demanded, her voice steady despite the fear gnawing at her insides. She didn't like when Demons called her. She was reminded of her time with Alastor and the feelings of helplessness and it chipped away at the confidence she typically presented at the Crossroads.

The Demon's grin widened. "A new player in the game," it replied cryptically. "One who wishes to discuss matters of great importance. Alastor's debts are of particular interest."

Without another word, the Demon vanished. Shay gripped Nero's mane, her jaw set with determination.

As the mist cleared, a figure became visible. Standing in the center of the road was a Demon unlike any she had seen before, tall with dark, leathery wings and eyes that glowed like molted gold.

"Hello, Shay," the Demon greeted, its voice smooth and malevolent. "I remember you from the black mansion. Lost my bid to that blubbering fool Krelp." His eyes roamed her body. "I should have bid higher. It's been too long since I laid my eyes on something so delectable."

The mere mention of Krelp made Shay want to vomit. She shivered, remembering his slimy tongue on her body and his teeth piercing her flesh. Shay squared her shoulders, refusing to show any sign of weakness. "What do you want, Demon?"

The Demon chuckled, a sound that sent a chill down

her spine. "I am Asmodeus," it replied. "And I seek to take over Alastor's skin trades. He is behind on his deliveries and his failures cannot go unpunished."

Shay's eyes narrowed. "And why involve me?"

Asmodeus stepped closer, his eyes piercing into hers. "Because you can help me and in return I will ensure your safety *forever*."

"That's not how this works," Shay said. "You ask for something, we make the deal."

Nero whinnied in reinforcement of what Shay had said.

Asmodeus stepped closer, the toes of his wingback shoes uncomfortably close to the rune. He leaned forward and whispered. "I heard a rumor about an aura–two auras really– that could be seen between realms." His hands flashed open. "Lit up the sky. The creatures who crossed the Veil can't stop talking about it. There's so much excitement and questioning and *want*!"

"I don't know what you're talking about," Shay said as Nero tipped his head down, ready to breathe fire and burn up Asmodeus for merely mentioning the auras.

A sinister smile split Asmodeus' lips. "Your Demon horse walks the Earthen plane, I'm sure not much happens there without you both knowing."

"The Earthen plane is quite large," Shay said as Nero fidgeted, moving two steps within the rune circle. "Plenty goes on without our knowledge."

"If you say so," Asmodeus said.

"Present your ask or we're leaving." Shay was fed up with the amount of time the Demon was wasting.

"I want the skin trades of Hell."

Shay shook her head. "Can't do that. Alastor and the skin trades are tied up with another Crossroads deal."

Nero whinnied in agreement, wary of the Demon.

Asmodeus's brows rose with this revelation. The gold rings and chains of the Crossroads Demon glinted and caught Asmodeus's eye.

"How did you become the Crossroads Demon?" Asmodeus asked. "It's a powerful position for a human."

Shay stroked Nero's neck. "Nero is the real Demon. I'm simply his sidekick," Shay said.

Asmodeus studied the duo and Shay didn't like his gaze one bit. "We'll be in touch," Asmodeus said, scuffing his shoe across the markings on the road to release Shay and Nero, before walking backward into the mist and shadows.

Shay leaned down, doing her best to maintain composure. "Run," she whispered to Nero.

Nero shivered, controlling the urge to turn into something else knowing that the threat of Asmodeus was still nearby. He turned and galloped away.

Shay didn't like the prying questions from Asmodeus. And while she typically didn't tell Jed details about their Crossroads deals, she just might have to discuss this with him. If Jed was going to ensure she didn't fail at keeping Meg's children safe, he needed to be aware.

# THIRTY

ALASTOR'S HANDS CLAWED AT THE SCORCHED earth outside the castle in the burning caves, his nails breaking and fingertips bleeding as he dug deeper into the dirt. Flames danced around him, casting eerie shadows on his twisted, sweat-soaked face. He'd set the grass on fire burning blade and root to make the excavation easier. His breath came in ragged gasps, his heart pounding with desperation and madness.

"Where are they?" Alastor muttered through gritted teeth, his voice a hoarse whisper. "Where are the bones?"

*Find my bones. Find my bones. Find my bones!* Lucifer's voice in his mind was a relentless torment that had plagued him for too long. *Find the bones and release me!* Lucifer's voice echoed in Alastor's mind, dripping with malice.

Alastor's neck twitched and he longed to dunk his head under water to make his father's voice stop. His focus resumed by the frantic search. He had spent weeks combing all of Hell, driven by the singular need to find Lucifer's bones. His fingers scraped against something hard and unyielding, and Alastor's heart skipped a beat. With trembling hands, he brushed the dirt, revealing a small, gnarled bone–a little finger bone, barely longer than an inch. Easily missed when the Deacons collected Lucifer's bones after Meg had drained him of blood and he dropped to the ground as nothing but a skeleton.

A triumphant laugh escaped Alastor's lips, a sound that echoed across the castle grounds with a manic intensity. The Hellions working alongside Alastor stopped their digging and focused on him. As Alastor held the bone in his hand, a shiver ran down his spine. There was something unnerving about the bone, something ancient and powerful that seemed to pulse with a promise of life. Alastor's grip tightened, his knuckles white with exertion and anticipation.

*You found it! You found something of me. You must find the rest!* Lucifer chanted over and over again.

Alastor stood, a crazed grin twisting his lips as he made his way toward the castle. He shoved the bone into his pocket, the weight of it pressing against his chest like a talisman of power. A promise that this hunt was almost over.

---

IN THE DIMLY LIT BALLROOM OF the castle in the burning caves, Sparrow's eyes narrowed with suspicion as Alastor crouched beside the bathtub.

"I heard a rumor that you lost something," Sparrow approached Alastor as he rubbed a towel over his face. The poor Demon had just finished nearly drowning himself, again. Sparrow wondered how long the guy was going to go on like this.

Alastor scoffed. "I lost nothing." He paused to shake a finger in Sparrow's direction. "I take that back. The only thing I've ever *lost* has been Shay."

Sparrow rolled his eyes. "You never deserved that creature." He made his way to Alastor's map. "You lost Meg. Heard she was rebuilding a portal and went missing."

"No biggie," Alastor shrugged. "She won't come back. If she ever steps foot in Hell again, I'll make her wish she was never born." He patted his pocket. "I've found a bone. I'm nearly there. I just need the rest of Lucifer's bones and I'll be released from this chore."

Sparrow tapped the map with an index finger. "Your numbers linger further. You are far behind in delivering souls to me."

"You're not the only one who keeps bringing that up," Alastor snapped, his eyes wide and black, water dripping down his face. "I have quotas to reach but I carry this burden." His arms stretched wide as he motioned to the castle around him.

Sparrow's brows rose. "You know, Meg's soul would be worth a lot. A damn lot. Shame she's missing."

Alastor's body stilled as he stared at Sparrow. He finally moved, crossing the room to lounge casually on a leather chair, a smirk playing at the corners of his lips as he regarded his ally with cool detachment.

"Ah, she is a precious little plaything, that Meg." Alastor reached for a bottle of whiskey that was near the chair.

Sparrow's jaw clenched in frustration. "You owe me

souls. I'm tired of waiting." Sparrow's eyes narrowed, a spark of anger igniting within him. "Her soul could be used to pay off your soul debts. Her soul is worth more to you than anything else."

Alastor's demeanor shifted, his eyes glowing with interest. "I am not some lesser Demon to be threatened," Alastor said.

Sparrow met Alastor's gaze head-on. "We are bound by more than the soul trade," Sparrow reminded him. "You're a creature of greed and ambition. You'll do anything to get what you want." He motioned to the ballroom. "Look at you here. This is not a hovel in the mountains. Focus on a clear decision and stop making mistakes."

A tense silence fell over the ballroom as Alastor considered Sparrow's words, his expression unreadable. Then, with a slow, deliberate movement, he rose from the leather chair and stepped closer to Sparrow, his gaze piercing and intense.

"Lucifer is nothing more than a fallen Archangel," Sparrow said. "He is not God. He is merely bone and dust. His granddaughter killed him once already. She's killed other Archangels. Take a lesson from your niece and stop listening to that voice in your head."

"You may be right," Alastor conceded, his voice low and dangerous. "But remember this, Sparrow, I am the standing King of Hell," he patted his shirt pocket, "and Lucifer will heed my word when he takes the reins."

It was a good threat, maybe even a great one. But Sparrow had a history with Lucifer, and he wasn't afraid of the old crone. Sparrow knew things–better yet, he had a plan.

"If I help you find Meg, it will be on my terms, not yours. And you will owe me a debt." Alastor rubbed his chin, contemplating Sparrow's words.

Sparrow's jaw was set with determination as he took a step closer to Alastor. "Just tell me where she is."

With a smirk, Alastor leaned closer, his breath hot against Sparrow's ear. "She's in Hell," he whispered, his voice sending a lick of fire down Sparrow's spine. "And if you want to find her, you'll have to go through me first."

Sparrow's hand curled into a fist and he refrained from punching a hole in Alastor's chest and ripping out his still beating heart. He could do it. He should do it. Shadows gathered at Sparrow's feet and his wings pulsed open.

Alastor smirked and backed away. "The Hellions will find her eventually. But you are more than welcome to search."

Sparrow gathered himself and backed away. "Be careful, Alastor," Sparrow said from the shadows. "One day you might dip your head in that tub and it will be flame, not water."

# THIRTY-ONE

NERO STOOD AT THE OPENING OF THE CORRIDOR that led to the back exit of the Peabody Library. He was waiting for Jed to follow and unlock the door. But, Jed kept turning pages on his damned book and holding up a finger. Nero had half a mind to piss where he stood. Instead, he stomped his hooves and pawed at the floor, threatening to scratch it to pieces. He didn't care if the floor was painstakingly laid with turn of the century salvaged bricks sourced from Spain or hand scraped Elm wood. He'd destroy it in an instant if Jed didn't get off his ass. Nero finally released a whinny of annoyance. Maybe he'd blow fire from his throat, just a little bit, enough to burn the book Jed was reading.

"Jed!" Shay shouted across the room. She was holding a spatula and had stepped out of the kitchen.

Jed pushed his chair back and stood. "Fine. Fine."

"You wanted a dog while we were living in Hell," Shay said. "You can't even let out the horse when he needs to go.

A dog needs to go out even more frequently." She shook the spatula at him.

"Who the hell has the chore of *letting the horse out to pee* in the history of ever?" Jed snapped back.

"Be thankful you're the first." Shay stood, eager to fight. She was antsy and they'd all been cooped up inside for too long. Everyone was getting on each other's nerves. The horse, the adults, the kids... the Hellion who was currently rearranging boxes in the attic.

Nero turned as Jed got closer and nodded toward the corridor over and over again, huffing and snorting and tapping his hoof on the floor.

"Yes. Yes," Jed said, his fingertips tingling with energy. He passed Nero and strode down the corridor.

Nero trotted after him, nickering and whinnying. He was making a fuss and he knew it. How dare Jed make him wait, Nero was a Crossroads Demon for Christ's sake!

Jed cursed as he unlocked the door that led to the empty lot and scraped his foot over the runes and lines of salt so Nero could pass. The horse was, after all, a Demon. He didn't belong on the Earthen plane. But since he was tethered to Shay, he had to stay. He wanted to stay because each time Nero was gone, Shay managed to get kidnapped by a Demon.

Jed shoved the door open and walked out first. Nero followed close and bit Jed's shirt, snapped his teeth together and made a hole. That was for making him wait.

Jed swatted at Nero. "Hey. Hey!"

Nero whinnied lightly and trotted away. Jed would find the hole when he changed his clothes. Nero whinnied to himself in laughter; serves Jed right. Next time, Nero might kick over the table.

"Stay close," Jed warned.

Nero wandered the empty lot, wary of the shadows beyond the property and swell of the river. Jed began patrolling the exterior of the lot, checking his wards, and stooping to draw new ones.

"Stay away from the perimeter," Jed warned.

Nero glanced at him, then the markings on the cracked pavement next to him. He needed to get out, he needed to make it back to Hell and find Meg. A long time ago Nero had decided most humans were good for nothing and stupid. No wonder they couldn't find her. Nero wanted nothing more than to see Rue and Remington happy again. The children needed their family, they didn't belong trapped indoors for all this time. He could find Meg and help put an end to this, he just knew it.

Nero stood at the edge of the property. He glanced at Jed. The man wasn't paying attention to him.

Nero found a stick and picked it up between his teeth. He walked to the edge of the lot and scraped the stick over the runes, breaking the wards.

"Hey!" Jed shouted, the shift in the protective dome was like a cool breeze blowing across the lot. "Nero," Jed warned. "What are you doing?"

Nero whinnied sadly, wishing he could have told Shay goodbye and promise he'd be back, but there wasn't time for that. He needed to go so Jed could fix his destruction on the runes. Nero leapt off the lot.

"Nero!" Jed shouted. "Where are you going?"

Nero ran down the street, his hooves clopping on pavement. He galloped around a truck, rounded a brick corner store, then made his way to a nearby park. He needed space to leap through the Veil.

There it was. He could see a sliver of reality wavering like heat waves on a sidewalk.

Nero found the split in the Veil and leapt through. The scent of woodsmoke and pine was faint. Nero glanced from side to side, the Patapsco River of Hell was eerily silent, a dark reflection of the Earthen plane. His eyes quickly adjusted to the ochre light that bathed the infernal landscape. He took a breath, steeling himself for the task at hand: finding Meg.

Nero tipped his head down and galloped. Hooves moving faster than lightning, he crossed empty cities and towns and crumbling roads until the once-familiar sight of the castle in the burning caves loomed in the distance. Smoke rose from the castle grounds. Nero's senses were on high alert. The distant sounds of wailing souls and the crackling of infernal fire filled the air. Nero slowed his pace coming through the surrounding forests, not wanting to be seen. He creeped his snout just beyond the shadows and saw the castle grounds were smoldering and lumps of dirt were everywhere.

Hellions, hunched and snarling, were scattered across the grounds, digging feverishly in the ashen dirt.

Nero's eyes narrowed as he recognized the figure overseeing the excavation. Alastor, the rat bastard. Nero held in a whinny of disgust, trying to stay hidden amongst the shadows. His throat ached to set the Demon on fire.

Alastor was barking orders at the new Hellions as their

claws and makeshift tools tore into the ground with frantic energy.

Nero moved closer, careful to stay hidden in the shadows cast by the twisted, gnarled trees that dotted the landscape at the edge of the forest. His heart pounded in his chest as he observed the scene, trying to make sense of what he was witnessing. Alastor's voice carried through the air, harsh and impatient all while he patted his shirt pocket as though something special were hiding between the cloth.

Nero would remember this. Whatever the Demon held in his pocket was important.

"Faster! We don't have all eternity!" Alastor snarled, his eyes blazing with manic intensity. "I need the bones! Keep digging!"

Nero's mind raced. So what the others had said was true; this was what Alastor was after, the remnants of Lucifer. Nero had never met the original fallen Angel, but he'd heard stories from Meg's Hellions. If Alastor succeeded, his power would be unimaginable.

Nero scanned the grounds, searching for any sign of Meg. He edged closer, staying within the cover of the shadows. He hadn't seen Meg since she arrived early that morning months ago to leave Rue and Remington at the library. Nero hadn't returned to Hell since before that time. The realm had a different vibe now, Nero could feel it in his bones. His teeth mashed together. He had to find Meg and get her out of here before Alastor's plan came to fruition. He took a step back, ready to slip away and continue his search, but a dry twig snapped under his hoof, echoing loudly in the still air.

Alastor's head snapped in his direction, his eyes

narrowing as he scanned the shadows. Nero held his breath, pressing himself against the trunk of a tree, praying he hadn't been seen, not that the tree could hide him.

"Who's there?" Alastor growled, his voice dripping with menace. "Show yourself!"

The Hellions paused their digging, their grotesque heads swiveling toward the source of the noise. Nero's heart pounded in his ears as he remained perfectly still, his eyes locked on Alastor.

After a tense moment, Alastor turned back to his minions. "Get back to work," he snapped. "We don't have time for distractions."

Nero exhaled slowly, relief flooding his veins as he backed away, deeper into the shadows under the cover of the trees. He had to find Meg, and quickly. Every second in this Hell was not good. He didn't want to be there himself. This was worse than when the Raven King was walking the Earthen plane. Whatever Alastor was, unseating Meg from the throne was causing a massive disturbance.

Nero backed out of the forest and turned as he reached the road. One hoof hit the pavement and the sound echoed louder than he'd ever remembered. He stepped down with as second hoof and the ground reverberated as though he'd stomped with all his strength. Yes, Hell had changed. Before the realm had welcomed him with open arms, let him swim in the shadows and meld with the ochre sky, now it rejected him. It was as though with the changing of the throne Hell required its inhabitants to be *revealed*.

Alastor shouted in the distance.

Nero heard the sounds of dozens of footsteps running. He turned. Now, Nero had seen the dead walk in Hell, it was just the way this realm functioned, but they were typically slow and meandering. Nero looked toward the footsteps. These dead were not slow, they were fast.

Nero turned tail and ran. He felt a sharp tug as something grabbed his tail. Nero whinnied, eyes went wide as he turned and found one of the Fast-Dead gripping his tail and reaching for his rump. Nero kicked his back legs and bucked, trying to loosen the dead creature that was hanging on for dear life. He felt the bones of the dead man crack and break but it didn't let go.

Nero wasn't one to panic, but he'd never seen dead like this before. As he struggled with the clinger, more darted toward him. Nero's mind raced—he needed to escape the dead.

He took off galloping at a rapid pace, swinging his backend and kicking, trying to release the grip of the dead that had a hold on him. As Nero ran, he kicked and the body flopped like a crash test dummy, shredding it at the hips as the lower half of it dropped onto the ground. Nero glanced back, relieved that the fast-dead's mouth had been damaged and its jaw was missing. He wouldn't be bitten, he just needed the damn thing to get off his back. The creature reached up with its free arm and gripped the base of Nero's tail, dragging himself up. Nails bit into Nero's backside as the Fast-Zombie tore at his skin and dragged his body up more. Nero shook as he ran, trying to get the dead thing to drop off him but it was holding tight.

Nero ran harder, faster, rubbed against tree trunks to try and scrape the thing off. Soon the rushing of water distracted him. This was a familiar place. Thunder rumbled in the sky and raindrops fell. Hellsky was shrouded in storm clouds. Past the rows of trees he recognized the pond in the forest.

*Plip plop, plip plop.* Nero recognized that dreaded sound. The hallowed call of the Nightjar. He was in Demore's forest and she was nearby.

Nero wished the Basilisk was still in Demore's pond. He would consider jumping in there to get free of the dead man crawling on his back.

The creature slammed its nails into Nero's flank. Nero whinnied in pain as the zombie dragged itself up his back. He sideswiped the trees, bouncing side to side trying to scrape off the half zombie like sidewalk gum on his hoof. But the creature swung with his movement. I crawled further up his back, nails digging into the sensitive spine at the base of his neck. Nero reared up and whinnied violently.

The plip-plop sound was closer, hovering nearby. Nero looked up to see the wraithlike blackened tendrils of her figure gliding toward him.

"My precious. My baby. My gift," her voice whispered in mournful melody. "What have you brought me?"

Nero scraped against the widest tree trunk he could find, ready to drop to the ground and roll to get the creature off.

"My precious. My baby. My gift." Demore was closer now.

The rainfall intensified until Nero could see her clearly. He whinnied in both pain and begging.

"A horse, of course a horse, my baby," Demore sang to a tune of her own. "What have they done to you?"

Abruptly, Demore's wailing cry turned into a scream as

she reached down and grabbed the dead man clawing at Nero's back. She tore the creature off Nero, flew above the treetops and flung the half of a dead man across the forest toward the castle grounds, releasing a wail of disgust as she did it.

Nero slumped against trees and lowered himself to the ground. The Fast-Zombie had torn his back open and he oozed blood. He held in all sound for fear of getting the attention of more of the fast dead.

Demore drifted down from the forest canopy. *Plip-plop, plip-plop*, her hallowed call softened as she approached the injured horse. "What have they done to my baby?" she lowered her wraithlike form to the ground and draped her shadows over him. "I'll take care of you my baby," Demore purred, rubbing her face on his neck.

Doom flooded Nero, he didn't have time for this creatures' shenanigans. But... his body did hurt and he was bleeding. Maybe she could help him, just until the wounds were a little better.

# Thirty-Two

Two things happened that caused Jed to rethink every decision he'd ever made these past few weeks. Jed ran toward the break in the wards, sliding on his knees, crumbling cement tearing his skin, chalk in hand, ready to restore the runes. Then the door to the Peabody Library swung open. Rue stepped out. Her aura–although dimmed–shone through the break in the wards.

A shadow shifted beyond the runes of protection, paused to focus, and then flew over Jed's head into the warded lot, heading straight toward Rue.

Rue screamed at the top of her lungs as the bat-like Demon flew to her, slender arms and legs and talons out, ready to scratch and grab. Long teeth were ready to bite.

With one arm, Jed attempted to replace the rune. With his free hand, arcane magic rushed from his fingertips as he spat words that sounded like a semi-truck smashing into a bridge. Before he could finish the rune, something slammed into his shoulder and sent him rolling onto his ass.

"Run, Rue!" Jed shouted as he scrambled to his feet.

More Demons were coming. They were rushing the break in the wards.

Rue turned and ran for the door. With both hands she pulled hard and the heavy door squealed open. The Demon grabbed it with both hands and ripped it off its hinges, tossing it aside before following the girl. Bright light shined from the corridor with the door off its hinges, drawing Demons from the river and surrounding city. They'd been lying in wait for a moment to slink in and sink their teeth into children.

Demons of all kinds rushed the lot, trampling Jed and each other. Undulating clouds and burnt-looking creatures never seen on the Earthen plane before advanced toward the opening to the library. Jed could hear Rue screaming, then he heard the aggressive roar of Chel.

Jed's heart pounded against his ribs as he stood. The wards that had protected them were shattered, and Demons poured through the broken defenses, their eyes gleaming with malice as they homed in on the light from the doorway.

With a determined snarl, Jed drew on archaic energy and lightning left his fingertips, striking the nearest Demon. The creature lunged at him, its claws slashing through the air. Jed ducked, rolling to the side before delivering a swift, upward strike that severed the Demon's head. The body crumpled to the ground, but there was no time to celebrate. More Demons were already closing in.

Inside the library, chaos reigned. Chel, Shay and the children were surrounded. Bookshelves lay toppled, and the floor was littered with torn pages and broken furniture. The library, once a haven of knowledge and safety, was now a war zone.

Chel fought fiercely, his eyes blazing with determination. His Hellion blade had been confiscated by Alastor, so the broken chair leg would have to do. He cut down each Demon that dared come too close to Rue and Remington. Shay stood beside him, her eyes glowing with an unearthly light as she brandished a fire poker from the nearby hearth.

Rue and Remington's faces were pale but their eyes fierce with determination. They weren't afraid to fight, they just didn't have any weapons on them. The children each picked up broken table legs, ready to use them as clubs.

Jed ran down the corridor, fighting his way through the Demons that were filtering in, his muscles burning with exertion. He could hear the sounds of battle inside the library, the shouts and screams of human and Demon and Hellion. Desperation fueled his every move. He couldn't let the Demons take Rue and Remington. He'd promised Shay she wouldn't fail.

Finally, Jed broke through the opening of the corridor and burst into the library, tendrils of dark magic oozing from his fingertips. Devastation greeted him. Chel was bleeding from a deep gash on his arm, but still fought with determination. Shay was a whirlwind of power, her dark energy cutting down Demons left and right. But there were too many of them. Jed joined the fray, his magic taking out a cluster of Demons.

"Where's Nero?" Shay asked, knowing the horse could fight with them, could burn them all and stop this madness.

"He ran off," Jed said with a grunt as he turned a batlike

Demon to ice. Chel slammed it with his wooden chair leg and it shattered, dead and gone.

"More like that," Chel urged. "It's working."

"Get back," Shay shouted, swiping her fire-poker toward a cloud-like Demon that was hovering over Rue.

The Demon said something to her in garbled Hellspeak and for a moment Shay wished she'd taken the time to learn the language.

Chel backed into Shay and began moving her and the children back toward the main entrance of the library. They were being overwhelmed, it was as though the Veil separating realms had split open inside the library with the number of dark creatures that were flooding in from the back corridor.

"We must run," Chel said. "Shay, take the children. We'll stay here and fight."

"No," Shay argued.

"There's too many," Jed agreed. "Run, Shay-baby." He paused and leaned into her, dropping a kiss on her head. "Run!"

"I won't leave you!" Shay argued.

Jed was using so much magic his blue aura was lighting up the room. He had a few more spells in his pocket, but he didn't want to hurt Shay or the children if he used them. He needed them to go.

"I'll find you," Jed promised. "Please, run!"

"Now," Chel shouted. "Before it's too late."

Shay had a sickening feeling in her stomach. She didn't want to leave either of them. They were in this mess together. Emotion swelled in her chest. She didn't want to go.

Rue screamed as a tiny Demon clung to her leg and tried to bite her. Shay stabbed the creature through with her fire-poker, then flung it aside. It hit the wall with a splat. Shay herded Rue and Remington toward the door.

Just as it seemed they'd be overcome and have to separate, a blinding light filled the room.

An Angel descended, his presence commanding yet puzzled. His wings spread wide, casting a golden glow over the chaotic scene. With a wave of his hand, the Demons were obliterated, their bodies disintegrating to ash. The Angel's eyes swept over the room, taking in the devastation and those who remained standing.

"What do we have here?" the Angel asked. "A Hellion. A Nephilim." He leaned to the side and focused on Rue and Remington. "Those two are something different." Then he stared at Shay. "And you're *barely* human."

Magic prickled in Jed's hands. He drew on it, ready to blast the Angel to another planet. He had zero trust for Angels of any kind. They'd only hunted and tried to kill him his entire life. He wouldn't let this one do the same.

"These children," the Angel said, his voice resonant and powerful, "who are they, and why do they bear such auras?"

Jed took a deep breath, his voice steady despite the turmoil and urge to kill. "They are under our protection. Their mother left them with us to keep them safe. We will protect them from everyone and everything, including you."

The Angel's eyes narrowed, his gaze shifting to Shay. Recognition flickered in his gaze and he took a step back. "You," he said, his tone wary, "are part Crossroads Demon. Somehow. But you weren't born that way."

Shay lifted her chin, her eyes defiant as she swiped blue hair away from her face. "Yes, I am."

The Angel took a step backward. "No deals." He shook his head.

"This is not a crossroads," Shay clarified. "But that doesn't mean I won't kill you." She tapped the fire poker on her palm menacingly.

The Angel crossed his arms and he gazed quickly around the room. "You're all leaving?"

"That seems the smartest choice," Jed said.

"Can I stay here if you're leaving?" the Angel asked. "I need a place to hide." The Angel was surveying the library. "And I get the feeling you all can't stay here, not after this." He opened his arms to the piles of ash all over the floor.

"We don't own this place," Jed warned.

"I'll take care of it," the Angel promised.

"I have never met an Angel that I've trusted," Jed said. "Why should I trust you?"

"I've already fixed the wards." The Angel moved his hands to his hips, real proud of himself.

"I think we should take the deal," Chel suggested. "This piece of flying garbage could fend off more Demons who come here looking for us."

"Hey!" the Angel shouted. "I offer help and you insult me?"

Chel shrugged, unafraid and unbothered.

"I apologize for my friend," Shay said. "But we have yet to meet an Angel who hasn't tried to kill first."

The Angel toed a pile of ash before focusing on Jed. "Not all Angels are of the old ways. Some of us just want peace, just like God intended."

"You can stay here," Jed finally said. "We'll collect our things."

The Angel smiled with relief. He turned his back to the grouping and began picking up pieces of the broken chairs and tossing them in the fireplace.

Jed turned to the others. "Pack. Quickly."

Chel didn't have much to bring besides clothing and he stole some knives from the kitchen.

Rue and Remington had their bags ready, they always did. They'd grabbed them off the foot of their beds and waited outside Jed and Shay's door.

Shay hefted her pack and pulled out a crumpled piece of paper from her pocket. She stared at Meg's handwriting.

"I don't know where we should go," Jed was saying as he collected bundles of sage, bags of sand and bones, and his notebook of spells. "I can't think of what would be the safest, maybe the mountains?" he sighed. "We are just so far away. It might be a battle to get there."

"Jed…" Shay began.

"At least we have a Hellion with us. He'll help. He's already helped." Jed ran hands through disheveled hair before opening a drawer and pulling out a knife carved with runes. "I'll have to make more of these. One for everyone."

"Jed…" Shay was reading the note over and over again, an idea blossoming.

"We can avoid the big cities, but the Veil is thinning. The dead might start walking again like they did when Sparrow was wandering this plane." He sighed and closed his eyes, memories of the zombie apocalypse coming; the Lame Deer Casino, seeing Shay for that first time, French toast. His eyes flashed open.

"What if we went somewhere sunny?" Shay asked. "You know, a place where the sun was so bright it would be hard to see Rue and Remington's auras. The tattoos and the sunshine might be enough to hide them."

Jed contemplated. "I guess it could work." He turned to face Shay.

She was holding up Meg's note with an address written on it. "How do you feel about Florida?"

# Thirty-Three



*Meg*

I DREAM OF SKEELE. Of his bare skin sliding against mine, fingers pressed into my hips, gripping horns in ecstasy, the feel of him inside me as I take what I want, my mouth pressed to his neck, sharp teeth biting. The smooth taste of his blood, the deep moan in his throat as he lets me take my fill before sinking his teeth into my wrist. He likes it like this, watching me ride him while he eats, blood dripping down my lips, the motion of us. It's always been like this, slow yet frantic. His patience, my lack.

It all ends too quickly and I wake up with my teeth pressed to something soft, searching for blood. My eyes flash open as cotton fills my mouth.

I've bitten a pillow.

A pillow?

I scramble upright, kicking the blanket off myself. My

feet hit the floor and I back away from the bed until my spine hits a wall.

Where am I?

I blink rapidly, clearing the sleep from my eyes and give my brain a moment to catch up. The sharp pain of my broken wing pressing against the wall helps bring me back to reality.

Where am I?

There are no windows, stone walls, and a solid door. I cross the room and try the handle. It's locked. There's another door. I cross the room again and open it. A bathroom. A real bathroom with a shower and everything.

I turn and stare at the bed. There's four pillows and heavy white linens. Like a hotel. This can't be a hotel. How did I get here? I scan my body, my arms and legs. I'm clean and wearing black sweats and thick socks. Who washed me? Who dressed me?

No no no, this can't be good. I tap my knuckles on the walls, trying to get a sense of weakness or something hidden. There are no decorations, just white paint. I notice a dresser. I open all the drawer and find clothes. Crazy person clothes, just sweats and granny panties and sports bras. What the fuck who dresses like this? I try the door again, remembering the stories Shay told me about the black mansion and rich Demons searching for blood and sex. Maybe that's where I am; bound for destruction, locked in this room, awaiting a fate worse than death. I should have killed Alastor the moment Shay told me the Demon was still alive but I was trying to be better. I was trying to channel compassion. Look where it got me.

There's an ache in my thigh and I remember cutting off

the birthmark. I pull my pants down and get a look at the healing wound. I'm surprised that it didn't fester since the knife was probably dirty and my makeshift bandage was nothing but filthy clothing. There's just bright pink skin where the ouroboros used to be. I stare, never having seen my thigh without the strange birthmark.

Something shifts in my stomach. Wetness drips from my ears. My hands come away covered in dark blood that smells putrid. I stumble to the bathroom and vomit. This is the feeling I had after drinking the old blood that Alastor gave us. I search the bathroom cabinets for towels and wash the blood out of my ears and off my face. Then I crawl back into bed and close my eyes. I curl up and wrap my arms around my middle, hoping it will help the ache in my gut.

———

I'VE DECIDED I miss Florida. I miss hot summer days and sleeping in and eating fruit and bacon and drinking rum and cokes for breakfast, taking naps and staying up late into the night watching the stars and the moon as a hot breeze blew in off the Gulf. There was plenty of blood in Florida, plenty of homeless men and crackheads that no one would miss. I could eat forever in Florida.

"Those thoughts are what got you on Heaven's naughty list," I mutter to myself since there's no one else to speak to in this room.

I'm not sure how much time has passed, but I've slept most of it as the feeling begins to consume me again. It's easy to drift into darkness here; the bed is soft, the sheets are warm, and the more I sleep the better the ache in my stomach feels. But not the ache in my heart. Nothing can help that. I'm beginning to wish Sparrow had just cut it out of me so I'd never have to deal with it.

This time when I close my eyes, someone is waiting for me. She has long brunette hair cascading down her back and her eyes are bright and just as green as they ever were. She whistles a light melodic trill.

I purse my lips, ready to whistle back, but she interrupts me.

"I spoke with Shay," Nightingale says. "Chel showed up wherever they are, missing a hand." Her head tips to the side, a very birdlike quirk. "Where are you, Meg?"

"I don't know." I tell her about the room, about being dragged through the portal and going unconscious. "I have no idea who has me but they gave me a bathroom and a..." Hot tears prick behind my eyes. I don't know how I feel about it after all those nights laying on the stone floor in the Helldungeon.

"A what?" Nightingale presses.

"A bed. Like a queen sized bed with pillows and blankets. It's like a hotel but I haven't seen a single soul. There's no clock. I have no idea how long I've been here. All I do is sleep. I haven't had blood since Skeele died. I'm just so tired all the time."

"Oh, Meg..." Night's hope-filled expression drops. "I'm so sorry. I didn't know he died."

My chin quivers. Crying in my dreams feels just as real as crying in real life. I let the tears flow and the anguish come out in breathy sobs.

Nightingale feels solid in my dream as she wraps her

arms around me and holds me close. "I know you had a bond with him," she says, soothing.

"He deserved better," I say with a hiccup and wipe my face. "He was all duty and tradition."

"He loved you." Nightingale grips my hands and gives me a little shake.

"I know," I whisper because it feels so wrong that I let him love me like that. "I took everything from him... his life. He died because of me."

"Tell me the truth," Nightingale is staring into my eyes. "You did not kill him. Who killed him?"

I nod and tell myself to agree with her. "Alastor did it."

"Are you in Hell?" she asks.

"I don't know."

"What do you feel?"

"Nothing. It's not hot or cold. I smell nothing. I feel nothing. I hear no sounds in this room, only my own heartbeat."

"Are you being fed?"

"I can't remember." I smooth a hand over my stomach. "I can't remember eating anything."

"That's probably why you're so tired and sleeping so much." Nightingale rubs my arms. "You need to eat. You need blood."

I stifle a chuckle. "There's nothing in this room."

"Did you check under the bathroom sink?" Nightingale tips her head to the side, oh so birdlike.

"Who in their right mind keeps food under the bathroom sink?" I ask.

Nightingale shrugs. "I used to hide food there when my father locked me up."

"Sure, I'll check when I wake up."

Nightingale nods with a smile like we've just decided on something really important.

"Did you make it to safety?" I ask. "Is Thrush safe?"

Night nods. "Sparrow let us into his kingdom. We are safe. As safe as we can be now that Babylon thinks we've swapped alliances."

I pause. "Why would Babylon care? Do they know what's happening in Hell? Do they know about the Deacons?"

Nightingale's image fades and she looks away, behind her like someone is approaching. "I have to go, Meg." She hugs me quickly. "We'll find you."

My eyes flash open. The room is dark but there is a sliver of light shining under the door. And... two shadows, like feet. Someone is standing there, in front of the door, waiting patiently for me to open it. Jokes on them, it's locked from the outside. A dreadful sensation floods my stomach. Shit, *it's locked from the outside*. I sit up and brace myself for an intruder.

# THIRTY-FOUR

Nightingale observed from a distance as Thrush practiced with Sparrow's Legion, his battle movements fluid yet determined. She didn't trust anyone in this realm to leave Thrush alone for long. She knew what it was like to be a teenager in the Seven Kingdoms of Heaven, but at least her son wasn't locked away in a basement. She couldn't help but feel a swell of pride in her chest as she watched her son, his determination to learn the way of the Legion's Angel warriors, although he did look a bit out of place. As though the darkness of Hell clung to him, plenty stared. He was starting to change; his hair had lightened to a white blonde in the weeks that they'd been in Sparrow's Kingdom.

The sun was starting to dip lower on the horizon, casting long shadows across the training grounds. A faint noise caught Nightingale's keen ears, drawing her attention, a distant sound that sent a shiver down her spine.

Leaving Thrush to his training, Nightingale moved swiftly through the darkening forest, her senses alert for any sign of danger. As she rounded a bend in the path, she nearly collided with a figure emerging from the shadows–Sparrow.

"Raven King," Nightingale greeted him, her voice tight with concern.

"What are you doing roaming the forests this late?" Sparrow asked. He seemed agitated, his face flexed in concern.

The moment she recognized it, he set his expression placid.

"Whatever I'd like. I thought I heard something suspicious." Nightingale glanced behind Sparrow but it appeared he'd come out of the darkness and not off a veering path. "Can't be too careful with the Fast-Zombies on the loose again."

Sparrow's expression remained unreadable, his eyes betraying nothing as he regarded his sister.

Nightingale took a deep breath. "Have you heard anything about Meg?"

Sparrow's brow twitched.

"She's been missing for weeks now. No one knows where she is." Nightingale crossed her arms as the forest darkened. "Have you heard a whisper or a rumor of her whereabouts?"

"I haven't seen her. Don't think she'd enjoy seeing me much after... everything." His black wings twitched.

"We've lost touch. We used to be closer," Nightingale said, eager to get information from him.

"You chose Hell," Sparrow said.

Nightingale frowned, unconvinced by Sparrow's dismissive tone. "Something doesn't feel right," she insisted, her instincts screaming at her to trust her gut. "I haven't seen a Deacon in a long time. It just feels like... the *balance* is off. Can you go check on her? Maybe just from afar. She doesn't have to know."

But Sparrow merely shook his head, his gaze drifting as if he were already miles away. "I'm sorry, Nightingale," he murmured, his voice barely audible above the rustling of the leaves. "I have my own matters to attend to. You'll have to search for Meg on your own."

With a sinking feeling in her chest, Nightingale watched as Sparrow disappeared into the darkness, leaving her alone with her fears. She knew she couldn't rely on him for help, not when he was so intent on keeping his own secrets. Not when he was so intent on Meg's death.

Determined, Nightingale squared her shoulders and set off into the night, her heart heavy with worry. She would find Meg and help get her to safety, even if it meant facing the darkest corners of Hell itself.

———

NIGHTINGALE RETURNED to the training grounds to find Thrush collecting his belongings.

"You don't need to watch me so closely," Thrush mumbled as Nightingale approached him.

"I don't trust them," she said.

"They're harder on me when you are here." Thrush's body ached from the training he'd endured. He was sure there would be plenty of bruises coming to the surface. He felt like a punching bag. "I need you to stop hovering. I'm not a child anymore." He stormed around Nightingale, avoiding her and began jogging toward the path that led to the cabin.

It was hard enough learning how to fit in among a Legion of Angel warriors. Everyone knew that Nightingale had chosen Hell over Heaven. And there were no other kids in this realm. Thrush and Rue and Remington had been the first children born in a long time.

Thrush raised his arm and pulled a leaf off a branch overhead. He missed his cousins, hadn't spent a day without them since they were born. Now they were somewhere else and he was stuck in the Seven Kingdoms of Heaven. He couldn't even contact them since Meg had never disclosed their location. He hated it. He hated every second of this place. Thrush felt different here, and he could see it every time he looked in the mirror and saw his white-blonde hair.

Thrush tore up the leaf in his hand, shredded it to a hundred pieces.

"Did the leaf deserve that?" a dark voice asked from the shadows.

Sparrow stepped out and Thrush came to a stop.

"It looked at me wrong," Thrush said.

A smile quirked Sparrow's lip. "Stupid leaf." He motioned for Thrush to follow him. "Training is going well I hear."

"Yeah," Thrush replied, glancing at the tall figure walking next to him.

"I told them to take it easy on you."

Thrush scoffed. "Tell that to my liver."

Sparrow's brow rose in question. "I also told them you

might've been trained by the Hellions and to keep you on your toes."

"How do you know that?" Thrush asked.

"I was a Hellion." He paused for dramatic effect. "All males of the Archangel families are required to do their time as a Hellion. Did your mother not discuss this with you?"

Thrush shook his head.

"When the time comes, you must go. You must learn true darkness to rule in the light. You must see bad to do good. I have no children of my own. As the next in line for this kingdom, you must prepare."

"And if I choose not to go?"

"You will curse this bloodline again. You will go."

"Why?" Thrush pushed. "There are no more children. My mother told me that I was the first in decades. It was a miracle." Thrush didn't want to go back to Hell with Alastor in charge. He'd seen enough of Alastor's damage when on patrol with the Hellions. He'd heard the stories of what Alastor had done to Shay and Jed. "Doing time as a Hellion didn't make you good."

Sparrow turned to his nephew and found the boy glaring at him.

Shadows pooled at Sparrow's feet, threatened to go after the boy and drain air from his lungs, make him eat his tongue, make him listen to reason. Sparrow glared down at the boy. "You should go home. Now," he warned.

Thrush turned and ran.

# Thirty-Five

*Meg*


I DON'T THINK I'll ever get out of here. My throat is dry, my body weaker than ever. It's disorienting not having sunlight or a clock.

I know I will die soon. I will rot away. I will wake as a walking corpse, stuck like all the others now that the Deacons are gone. And if that happens, I will forfeit ever seeing my children again. My soul will be trapped. There is no balance any longer.

Crawling out of bed, I stumble into the bathroom. I open the cabinets under the sink again, checking for food like Nightingale suggested. There's nothing. There has been nothing for a long time. Not even a bug or a rat that I could eat.

I turn on the water and drink from the faucet. Water does nothing for me. I need blood. Fresh blood. Holding up my hand, I only see skin and bone. I trace the hollows of my cheeks in the mirror before staring. Dull eyes stare back at me.

This must end.

My eyes trace the edge of the mirror, could whoever trapped me in here be this stupid?

It's been a long time since I've given up completely, but I think my time has come. I have no one left. I scattered them all or they've died. This is not giving up though, this is taking control. I will not have my soul wander eternity in Hell, lost. I will not be one of the walking dead.

I punch the mirror over and over again until cracks form and it shatters, pieces fall on the countertop and into the sink. I pick up a large shard, testing its sharpness with my fingertip. It slices and blood blooms. I touch it to my wrist, press in and hiss, tears well in my eyes. The only way I'll ever see my children again is as a ghost, like Clea. At least I'll have that. Hell is lost and so am I.

I press harder until a stream of blood drips down my arm.

The door to the room slams open and heavy footsteps echo. Someone rushes in–a blur of black in my periphery. Strong hands grab both my wrists, shaking my right hand until I drop the shard of mirror. It shatters in the sink as blood drips off my elbow.

"It's kind of hard to be invincible together if you're dead, Meg," a familiar voice growls in my ear.

Sucking in a sharp breath, my blood runs cold. *No!*

*-until next time-*

# Temptations of Fate (Veil of Shadows 12) [Unedited]



## Chapter 1

*Then*

Sparrow was a fallen Angel turned Hellion turned walking dead turned Raven King. It wasn't all for nothing. He'd cleared his family curse by sacrifice. He'd done as instructed by the remaining Archangels. If he wanted his family land, he had to purify his blood. And hers. So he did it. The only way he could, he killed her. Stabbed her in the heart with a blade that made her bleed out every drop of his blood she'd ever consumed; it erupted from her body and killed her for twenty-four minutes. Their bond was severed. The problem was—not necessarily a problem because he'd sighed a breath of relief in private when he'd heard the news–she didn't stay dead for long.

## Chapter 2

*Now*

Sparrow held Meg's wrists, no more of her blood would be spilled. Not in his Kingdom. Nowhere else if he had a say in it. Meg's expression was one of horror and shock, as though she couldn't fathom a worse person to stop her from ending it all. Her body had turned to stone beneath his grip. Wide blue eyes stared up at him. Disheveled dark hair stuck to her lips and she was breathing erratically.

Sparrow released her wrists and stepped back. Hands up in surrender to show her he was safe. He wasn't sure she'd ever believe it, but the thing he'd done, he'd done for her, for *them*.

Meg moved faster than he'd expected in her weakened state. She grabbed another piece of the broken mirror and held the sharp fragment to his neck.

"What the fuck," she finally spit words like hate. "Where am I?"

Sparrow stepped back until his spine and wings hit the wall. She looked equal parts as though she might devour him with rage and collapse on the floor from exhaustion. It was the dead blood Alastor had fed her. Clearly it hadn't dissipated from her system even though she'd been sleeping for weeks.

"You're safe," was all Sparrow said.

"If you are here, I am not safe," Meg sneered. She'd cut her hand with the shard of glass she was holding to his neck and blood dripped down her thin wrist. "Let me go," she demanded.

"Can't do that." Sparrow took a side step toward the bathroom door. "I think you should lie down."

"Let me go," Meg demanded.

"Go lay down, Meg, before you fall flat on the floor."

Blood dripped and Sparrow stilled, scowling at her, annoyed that she didn't move, that she wouldn't listen to him.

"I will kill you," she threatened.

"Why would you want to do such a thing?" Sparrow took another step to the side.

Meg took a step forward. "Because you deserve it. Because of what you *did*." She stumbled and fell into the doorframe, her broken wing scraped the wall and she hissed in pain. "Because you *hurt* me." A broken heart was more than hurt. He'd scarred her to the core.

Sparrow didn't move to help her. Knew if he moved a muscle in her direction, she'd stab the shard of glass into his body. "You should go back to bed."

"You should shut the fuck up." Meg reached over her shoulder and pressed a hand to the broken bone that was sticking out of her wing. It would never heal with how badly it was damaged. She glanced toward the bedroom door. "Let me out of here."

"No." Sparrow took another step backward.

Meg's stomach growled, and it echoed throughout the room.

Sparrow glanced down.

"Don't look at me," Meg seethed.

"Lay down," he ordered.

"Fuck off," she snapped. She took a breath, collecting her energy, pushed off the door frame and took a step toward the Raven King, murder in her eyes. "I want out. Now."

"Nope." Sparrow shook his head.

"I…" The hate in Meg's gaze vanished as her eyes rolled to the back of her head and she collapsed.

Sparrow waited, ensuring she didn't wake, burst to her feet, and stab him in the neck. She wanted to. That was easy to see. He toed her shoulder with his boot. She didn't wake, moved little more than shallow breaths. Sparrow crouched and peeled her fingers away from the shard of mirror. He took it to the sink and collected the rest of the broken glass, wrapped it in a towel and set it outside the door to the room. He glanced at the bed, then to her limp body on the floor. She'd hate him for touching her, but he was going to do it anyway.

Sparrow stooped next to Meg and rolled her protecting her broken wing. He slid an arm under her shoulders, another under her knees and lifted. She was too light, nothing but bones, her cheeks gaunt. He wasn't so sure about Teari's recommendation of Tincture of Time for the dead blood to clear her system. Sparrow set Meg on the bed and looked her over. He got a cloth from the bathroom and cleaned the blood off her hand and wrist. He watched her thready breaths. A hand went to his pocket and fingers slid over the vial of blood. He'd been waiting for the right time to give it to her. He couldn't wait much longer for her to recover. Alastor was wreaking havoc on Hell and the

Earthen plane, they needed to put a stop to it, but they needed Meg well.

Sparrow took the vial out of his pocket, flipped off the cap and dripped the blood into Meg's mouth. Then he turned-tail and made fast work of getting out of her room. If she woke with fresh blood in her system, she'd probably have the strength to rip every feather off his wings. But Sparrow didn't feed her fresh blood. It was bagged like the Hellions would drink. Just enough to sustain her. He closed the door and locked it.

Picking up the towel filled with broken mirror, he made his way out of the bunker. He waited at the main door, listening closely to ensure no one was wandering the forest and might see him. Gabriel had taught Sparrow plenty, more than his own father. Always have a place to hide your people during disaster. When Angels had inhabited the Earthen plane thousands of years ago, they'd built shelter in the mountains to stay hidden and survive. The same kind of shelter worked well for Gabriel during the Fast-Zombie War, his kingdom survived most of the massacre, the other Archangels weren't so lucky. They didn't have a place to hide, thinking that the Seven Kingdoms of Heaven were completely safe. No realm was safe. And Sparrow was glad he'd heeded Gabriel's advice during the rebuild and constructed the bunker in the small ridge of mountain at the edge of his Kingdom.

After not hearing a thing, Sparrow opened the door and exited the bunker. He made his way to the main house and made a mental note to remove everything sharp from Meg's room. The flash of her teeth crossed his mind. He couldn't remove those, unfortunately.

The Legion were in the training yard, the rest of his staff busy with daytime duties. The walk to the main house was uneventful. Sparrow was glad he didn't run into anyone. He surveyed the path in the distance, hoping to not see the dark flash of Nightingale's hair as she hounded him. He couldn't really explain the towel he carried, filled with bloody shards of mirror. He made quick work of returning home and disposing of the mess.

# Chapter 3

The sun was setting as Jed drove through the sleepy town of Perdido Key. The sky was painted in hues of pink and orange across the horizon, a stark contrast to the darkness they had left behind.

Tires crunched over a seashell driveway as Jed pulled up to the small beach house. It was dark and quiet. He'd had driven all day and night, over fifteen hours through the Carolinas and Alabama. States none of them had ever been too and didn't have time to peruse. Each time they used a rest stop, Jed drew more runes on the Jeep Grand Cherokee that they were driving. He'd darkened the windows and carved a shrouding spell into the roof. He could never be too safe after the disaster at the Peabody library.

Shay reached for the door.

"Wait," Jed warned. "Let me check it out."

Shay sighed. "I'm sure it's fine."

"Listen to him," Chel grumbled from the cargo area where he was sitting. The Hellion barely fit. Shoulders hunched and wings awkwardly tucked away, Jeeps weren't designed for the comfort of a Hellion. "Believe me, if anyone wants out right now, it's me," he muttered.

Jed surveyed the beach house on Parasol Place. There were rocking chairs on the front porch and the yard was fenced. There was privacy and the soft sound of the ocean nearby was relaxing. He went to the front door, held his hand over the lock and whispered a spell. The door opened. Jed flicked on the lights and searched the house. He found nothing surprising. The beach house was small and simply decorated. It seemed too quaint for Meg's tastes and the lack of books would have them all going stir crazy. They'd have to find a library or bookstore. Satisfied with is findings, he made his way back to the Jeep.

Shay was watching him as he walked closer.

Jed decided he liked the way his boots crunched on the crushed seashells and the smell of the ocean air. He opened Shay's door and helped her out. "All clear." He smiled.

They all piled out, the sea breeze instantly wrapping around them. Shay took a deep breath, savoring the salty air. It was a new beginning, a much-needed respite from the chaos they had fled.

"Whoa," Jed stopped Chel. "We gotta do something about those wings."

"Who cares?" Chel looked around. "No one is here." He sniffed the air then his face twisted in confusion, there was no one for miles. He glanced at the nearby houses and apartments, not smelling any inhabitants.

Jed whispered a spell that hid Chel's wings from sight. "Come on, let's check out the beach," Jed said, a rare smile spreading across his face.

Rue and Remington ran ahead, their laughter echoing in the evening air. Chel followed, his eyes scanning their surroundings.

The light from sunset was so bright it hid their auras.

Shay and Jed walked hand in hand, the soft sand beneath their feet. The waves lapped gently at the shore, a soothing rhythm that calmed their weary souls.

Rue and Remington were splashing in the shallow water. Remington cupped his hands and shoveled ocean water at his sister as she shrieked in delight.

"This place is beautiful," Shay whispered, leaning into Jed.

"It is," he agreed, pulling her closer. "Their auras aren't like up north. The sun is brighter here."

"Hopefully the moon too." Shay kicked off her shoes and dug her toes into the soft sand. She'd never lived in a place that didn't require closed toed shoes or boots year-round. She had a sudden urge to buy flip-flops.

They stayed at the beach until the sky turned dark, the stars appearing one by one. And the moon was bright enough to hide the children's light.

Reluctantly, Shay called Rue and Remington out of the water and they made their way back to the house. Everyone was exhausted from the white-knuckled escape from Peabody library. They had been afraid of being attacked while they drove.

They made their way back to the house, their earlier excitement giving way to yawns and drooping eyes.

Inside, Shay was glad to find a room for the children and a master suite.

"I'll take the couch," Chel said, bending to look out the windows.

Jed and Chel secured the house, making sure all was safe. Marking the doors and windows with runes of charcoal and salt.

Shay helped the children get settled.

"I'm hungry," Rue said.

"Well," Shay said as she searched the cabinets. "There's not much here." She found bags of expired chips and cans of expired soups. "This stuff might still be edible." She piled the items on the counter and found plates and bowls. "We'll have to go to the store in the morning."

Remington was standing in front of the pantry. "There's a lot of soda here."

Silence fell on the group. Shay glanced to Jed.

"Has our mother been here?" Remington asked.

"A long time ago," Shay said.

Remington turned with cans of orange soda in his hands. He gave one to Rue with a look then passed the rest out.

"I'm sure she's okay," Chel said. "She has to be okay."

Cans popped open and Shay held hers up. "To bright sunshine."

"To sunshine," Jed echoed, a sense of hope filling the room.

For the first time in two days, they felt a sliver of peace. The road ahead uncertain, but for now they had each other and a place to rest their heads. And that was enough.

"Where is Nero going to sleep?" Rue asked.

Jed nearly spit soda mid-swallow. "If I see that horse again..."

"Hey," Shay argued. "Be nice. There was a reason for what he did."

"To get us all killed." Jed slammed his can down. "There was no good reason for what he did."

"Don't judge him so harshly," Shay said. "We don't know."

Chel grumbled something about stupid animals.

*

The morning brought heat and sun. Jed messed with the air conditioner, using more magic than handyman skill to get it working correctly.

"I want to go to the beach," Rue said. "It was so pretty last night. We've never been to the ocean before."

"Someone needs to go to the store," Shay said as she made a cup of coffee. Meg had an entire cabinet stocked with coffee. It was strange since she barely drank it in Hell.

"I can go," Jed offered. "You all can go to the beach."

The kids found shorts and T-shirts, Jed promised to look for swim suits while he was at the store.

"We are wholly unprepared for a beach," Shay said digging through her suitcase to find something. She settled on an old T-shirt and faded jeans and decided to sacrifice them to the cuts of scissors. "We need flip-flops, sunscreen, sunglasses, and hats."

Jed glanced at Chel. "I'm not sure they'll have your size in anything."

Chel looked up from his cup of black coffee and grumbled. "I'm not a beachy type of guy."

"You can't be going there in Hellion gear and combat boots." Shay was searching a hallway cabinet for towels. She found a stack, walked toward the front door, and motioned to the children. "Let's see if this daylight is enough."

Everyone filtered outside, shielding their eyes.

"It's a miracle," Jed said, staring at the children. "Not a spec of aura."

It was true. The Florida sunshine was so bright there was no aura visible. What little they'd seen last night was completely bleached out by the sun's rays.

# From the Author

Ahhhhh, I can't believe I left you hanging like that! The audacity.

Well, the good thing is that book 12 is coming shortly. Make sure you're signed up for my blog/website and never miss a new release.

I love hearing from readers, please send a note to meredith (at) mrpritchard (dot) com or contact me at my website.

Happy Reading!
-Meredith

# About the Author

M. R. Pritchard delves into the profound clash between good and evil, the mystical realms of gods and monsters, and the intricate transformations of ordinary people into beings of immense power. Her gripping narratives often unfold within the haunting backdrop of apocalyptic or post-apocalyptic landscapes, offering a unique blend of suspense and wonder.

M. R. Pritchard is a two-time Kindle Scout winning author, her short story "Glitch" has been featured in the 2017 winter edition of THE FIRST LINE literary journal. Her short story "Moon Lord" has been featured in Chronicle Worlds: Half Way Home (Part of the Future Chronicles) and will be time capsuled on the moon on the Lunar Codex in 2024.

Visit her website MRPritchard.com and Subscribe. You'll get subscriber only content, deleted scenes, updates, special previews of new projects, and book deals.

# Also by M. R. Pritchard

Other Books by M. R. Pritchard


<u>Science Fiction/post-apocalyptic:</u>

The Phoenix Project

The Reformation

Revelation

Inception

Origins

Resurrection

The Phoenix Project Compendium Edition

The Safest City on Earth

The Man Who Fell to Earth

Heartbeat


Asteroid Riders Series

Moon Lord

Collector of Space Junk and Rebellious Dreams


<u>Steampunk:</u>

Tick of a Clockwork Heart


<u>Dark Fantasy:</u>

Veil of Shadows Series:

Sparrow Man

Nightingale Girl

Scarecrow

Raven King

Nightjar

Night Owl

Etched in Darkness

Embrace the Night

Shadows of Destiny

Midnight Serenade

Echoes of Treachery


Thread the Bone


<u>Fantasy/Fairy Tale Love Story/Romance:</u>

Muse

Forgotten Princess Duology

Midsummer Night's Dream: A Game of Thrones


<u>Poetry/Short Stories</u>

Consequence of Gravity